D0929089

TEXAS GUNS

Jim Rimbow rode into the helltown he'd sworn to tame—a border-jumping, man-killing starbuster with a dying lawman on his backtrail. But Rimbow was gunning for more than glory. Rawhide tough and lawless, he meant to brace the range bawd whose kiss had killed his best friend—and slam a Texas answer at the gunfast cohorts whose hot bullets whispered "Live fast, Rimbow—for you won't live long!"

TEXAS GUNS

Leslie Ernenwein

GUNSMOKE

9/09 QQ 6/09-5
4-10 LAD 1-10 6(0)

This hardback edition 2005
by BBC Audiobooks Ltd
by arrangement with
Golden West Literary Agency

ISBN 1 4056 8033 4

British Library Cataloguing in Publication Data available.

All characters in this work are fictitious, and any resemblance
to persons living or dead is coincidental.

Printed and bound in Great Britain by
Antony Rowe Ltd., Chippenham, Wiltshire

Contents

To:

Doc Carter

. . . who likes to read western novels and ride western trails

TEXAS GUNS

1

JIM RIMBOW came out of the bleak Sonora hills at noon, crossing the Mexican border into Arizona by way of a trackless, brush-tangled canyon. Lack of sleep had turned his eyes bloodshot and a five-day growth of black whiskers masked his angular, gaunt-cheeked face. His leather vest and bullhide chaps bore the scars of long usage and bachelor patches showed in both sleeves of his faded cotton shirt. To look at him, he was a hungry drifter, but riding the grubline was farthest from his thoughts. Eleven hundred dollars in double-eagles were tightly wedged between the two-ply leather of his vest.

Aware of the gold's weight now, Jim Rimbow thought, *More money than I've ever had at one time. Or Mike either. . . .* A man doesn't come by big money polishing his pants in a cavalry saddle, or wearing a town marshal's badge, or trying to turn a homestead claim into a cow outfit. In all his thirty-one years Jim Rimbow had never possessed more than seven hundred dollars cash at one time.

Smilingly, in the way of a man savoring a fine realization and accustomed to speaking out in his loneliness, he said, "Eleven hundred gold."

9

It had taken some getting. And some sweating. The kind of sweat that dribbles from a man's armpits when the odds pile up and apprehension is a slugging fist in his belly. . . .

Keeping his sorrel gelding at a walk. Rimbow peered ahead with a squint-eyed wariness, his right hand close to holster. The past four months had marked him so that he apeared older than his years. Those months had revived a habitual vigilance out of his past—they had turned him spooky so that now, as a jackrabbit bounced up close beside him, Rimbow drew his gun with the instinctive speed of a man keyed to hair-trigger reaction. He cursed and said, sighing, "Good thing I'm quitting."

A man could take just so much of border-jumping. There was a limit to how long he could stand the pressure of hiding by day and riding by night, of cooking frugal meals over near-smokeless fires and rationing water by the drop. After that limit was reached the pressure did things to him, inside. He got to looking over his shoulder while he drank his coffee, and waking up with a gun in his hand. The thought came to Rimbow now that he had been lucky, luckier than a cross-eyed hunchback. Six gun-running trips into Sonora for Jube Tanner and he was alive to tell about it. By God, that was something!

He grinned, thinking of the close call he'd had this trip when the *rurales* almost cornered him in the brush beyond Barranca Prieta. Lady Luck had had her arm around him for certain, had hugged him tight while blind bullets tried to find him. And there was another time when he'd been chased by what seemed like half the *federalista* cavalry. He'd got a slug crease square across the belly that night, just deep enough to mess up his underwear. The wound hadn't hurt any at the time and not much, later, but the next morning, after it was all over, he had puked like a poisoned pup.

The gold had taken some getting for a fact. But he was shut of the deal now, or would be, as soon as he settled up with Jube Tanner. He thought contentedly, *If I never have to fire a gun again it will be a month too soon. . . .*

The sorrel rimmed out on a bald slab-rock crest, and here Rimbow halted, taking his long look at Tanner's Trading Post, which lay on the greasewood-dotted flats directly below him. Intently, with a thorough regard for small details, he considered the old adobe house with its trash-littered backyard and mesquite corral. Three of the four penned horses were familiar to Rimbow—Tanner's dun gelding, a brown mare and her suckling colt. It was the fourth animal, a bay with black points, which attracted Rimbow's attention. The bay hadn't been there ten days ago, and that saddle on the kak pole wasn't Tanner's centerfire rig.

Might mean something, Rimbow thought.

The bay's owner hadn't just stopped by for a sack of tobacco, or a drink of Tanner's diluted trade whiskey. The fact that he had gone to the trouble of unsaddling and penning his horse showed that he intended to spend some time at Jube's place.

Who was he? And why had he decided to stop over at Tanner's store?

11

A man would have to be hard up to spend the night at Tanner's. Jube wasn't much of a cook; beef and frijoles was the usual fare. That and jack rabbit stew. The man who owned that bay and the saddle would know about camping out. Rimbow nudged his gun loose in its half-breed holster and waited another five minutes before sending his horse down the slope. That strange bronc in the corral might not mean a thing, but the rough-and-tumble years had put an abiding cynicism in Jim Rimbow. Mistrust of men's motives was his habit, as much a part of him as the trooper-straight way he sat a saddle. A man's past fashions a certain pattern and makes marks on him that don't rub off. So it was now.

Rimbow rode into the yard with a premonition of trouble building up in him. But he grinned at the ponderous, flabby-faced man in the store doorway and said, "Well, I made it again."

"Where's your pack mules?" Jube Tanner asked.

"I told you it was to be my last trip," Rimbow said, easing back in saddle but not dismounting. "Sold the mules along with the Winchesters."

Then he inquired casually, "You got a visitor, Jube?"

"Whatever gave you that notion?" Tanner demanded.

Rimbow glanced at the corral, whereupon Tanner said, "By God, you notice things!"

"Sure," Rimbow agreed. "That's why I'm still breathing."

"You're spookier'n a female with fleas in her bustle," Tanner said derisively.

"I am for a fact," Rimbow agreed. "That's why I'm

12

quitting." He glanced at the bay in the corral and said, "Fair looking pony. Might have some Copperbottom in him."

"Well, a feller practically gave him to me," Tanner said, smiling blandly. "The bay went lame and this galoot was in a big rush. He took the next stage to Tombstone."

"So?" Rimbow mused, and understood that Jube was lying, and wondered why.

A man wouldn't be likely to leave a good saddle like that one on the kak pole. He'd be apt to take it along with him on the stage, unless he got a real good price for it. And Jube, who had no use for an extra saddle, wouldn't pay a good price. There was something wrong here, for certain.

"Did Captain Cortaro pay off in gold again, like he promised?" Tanner asked. His deliberately casual voice fanned Rimbow's increasing suspicion, for Jube seldom spoke casually of gold. It was the one thing he cherished. Jube seemed to have no need for women, and no real taste for whisky, or good food. But gold he dearly loved.

Rimbow nodded. He glanced past Tanner, and seeing that the plank bar was deserted, wondered if the bay's owner was waiting in the back room. That, he supposed, was the way a deal like this would be handled. If it was a deal.

"Eleven hundred dollars gold in one chunk," Tanner said. "And you're quitting a game like that? You must've been dropped on your noggin when you was a baby."

Rimbow grinned, as if deserving the censure and

13

accepting it. But he guessed the reason Tanner was talking so loud and thought, *Loud enough for a man in the backroom to hear....*

"Well, why don't you get down?" Tanner asked.

It occurred to Rimbow that he could ride out of here now with a fair chance of getting past gun range before a bullet reached him. But he had almost five hundred dollars more coming to him. Each of the six trips had given him a profit of better than two hundred dollars. Even though he might have to outshoot a would-be robber to get it, he wanted that money—he had sweated enongh for it. So thinking, Rimbow dismounted, taking care to keep the doorway in sight as he stepped down.

"Ain't you going to unsaddle and stay the night?" Tanner asked.

Rimbow shook his head. "Just long enough to settle up and buy a little grub for the trip to Reservation. I can make ten, fifteen more miles before sundown."

Tanner frowned. "You must be in a hell of a hurry," he complained. "You got a woman waiting for you in Reservation?"

"No, nor anywhere else," Rimbow muttered.

"Well, if it ain't some particular female you got your mind on, why don't you ride up the road to Tombstone tomorrow and get your needings in one of them straddle houses. That'd be a shorter trip than Reservation, and you might decide to come back for another run across the line—after you went broke in Tombstone."

"I've got no itch for a woman," Rimbow said.

"Then what's all the damned rush about?"

Rimbow shrugged. "It's rightly none of your business,

Jube, but I'll tell you anyway. I've got a pardner who's been holding down our little outfit alone the past four months." Thinking how it would be when he told Mike O'Mara that their money troubles were over, Rimbow added: "He'll be some pleasured to see me."

"One more day shouldn't make no difference to him," Tanner suggested. "He's probably not lacking for company. The new railroad building through Apache Basin has turned Reservation into a regular boom camp from what I hear. They say it's a tougher town than Tombstone."

"So?"

"You'd better unsaddle and rest your pants a spell," Tanner said. "Can't you be sociable with a man?"

This show of hospitality convinced Rimbow that there was something snaky here. Jube Tanner didn't give a damn for any man's companionship. All the trader wanted was money. Easy money. It occurred to Rimbow that the bay's rider might be waiting in the barn, which would explain why Jube wanted him to unsaddle his horse.

He shook his head. "Just a little grub, and the money you're holding for me, Jube."

Reference to the held money seemed to irritate Tanner. He said sourly, "You had damned little cash when you came here. For a man that's prospered like you have I'd say you're downright unsociable." He turned and walked into the store.

Rimbow trailed him, taking particular notice of the blanket-draped doorway to Tanner's living quarters at the rear. If he stood a trifle sideways at the bar he

15

could watch that blanket. The feel of an ambush grew stronger in him, though he couldn't yet guess from what direction the trap would be sprung.

He was within a few steps of Tanner, following him toward the bar, when the trader turned abruptly to the left. In the same instant a gun began blasting behind him, and Rimbow felt the smashing impact of bullets against his back. He attempted to draw his gun, but the bullets were like clubs beating him down. Swift, hard blows that paralyzed him.

The surprise of it exploded into pain. Vaguely, as from a far distance, Rimbow heard Tanner yell. He heard the gun blast again.

Then the floor's dusty boards thudded against his face.

When the westbound stage stopped on the crest of Spanish Divide to give the panting teams a rest, Deputy Marshal Jeff Halliday stepped down to stretch his legs. This was about six miles east of Tanner's Trading Post, and the lawman asked, "Isn't there a short cut to Reservation from Tanner's place?"

The driver nodded. "Horseback trail that saves better'n seventy miles."

Halliday scanned the sun-baked land ahead for familiar landmarks. His blue eyes held a faded, washed-out look, and what hair showed beneath the brim of his Stetson was bleached to tarnished silver, but his high-beaked face retained the same shrewd alertness which had caused men to call him "Hawk" fifteen years ago.

And they still did, with the same mingling of fear and respect in their voices.

"I used to know my way around this end of Arizona," Halliday said. "Punched cows for old Sam Chastain before I took up the law business."

"Reckon that was before Riley Jardine moved into Apache Basin," the driver suggested.

Halliday nodded. "Chastain had the country all to himself from Reservation clean to the Dragoons."

"Country's buildin' up," the driver said. "That new railroad will bring folks aplenty."

"Shouldn't wonder," Halliday agreed, and climbed back up to the high seat. As the driver eased his six-horse hitch down the steep grade, the lawman said, "I'd save upwards of two days by borrowing a horse from Tanner and taking the short cut."

"Don't reckon Jube would lend a horse, but he might rent one. He's quite a hand to collect the cash, Jube is."

"So I've heard," Halliday said, and dug out a stubby-stemmed briar. "I've also heard that Tanner might know who's running guns into Sonora for the rebels."

"That wouldn't be why you're in such a sweat to reach Reservation," the driver said, still careful not to ask the question. He glanced at Halliday and found the lawman giving his full attention to tamping tobacco into the briar.

Presently, when Halliday had the smoke drawing to suit him, he said, "I hear there's been some trouble between Sam Chastain and Riley Jardine."

The driver nodded. "But I didn't suppose the U. S. Marshal's office interfered in things like that."

17

"It doesn't."

"Then that ain't why you're here either."

There was a plain note of curiosity in the driver's voice, but Halliday ignored it. He asked, "What's behind the trouble?"

"Well, from what I hear it's the same old story. Two big outfits needing the same grass. Riley Jardine has been building up to this thing for five years. He helped Pinky Weaver get elected sheriff and knows Pinky won't interfere when the showdown comes. During the past month Jardine has imported some border riff-raff, they tell me. Real gunslingers that make it look bad for the Chastain outfit. They say Jardine's bunkhouse is a regular renegades' roost now, with half the Texas wild bunch on his Circle J payroll."

"So I've heard," Halliday said, "and that's why I'm heading for Reservation."

The stage driver loosed a sigh. "You sure had me guessing," he admitted. "Have you got some certain renegade in mind that might be there?"

Halliday nodded, but he didn't mention a name.

2

Gallows Company

For a queerly blank interval Jim Rimbow heard nothing and felt nothing. Then, as his shocked senses cleared, he became aware of Jube Tanner's voice. But Jube wasn't talking. He was groaning.

That seemed odd to Rimbow. What would Jube be groaning about? Rimbow opened his eyes. The big trader sat with his back to the bar, both hands pressed against his bulging belly. Blood dribbled redly between his fat fingers. It formed a soggy pattern that grew larger across the front of his shirt and below the belt buckle of his pants.

That didn't make sense to Rimbow either, until he moved, and a sharp shaft of pain ran up across his left shoulder. Then he remembered the shooting. Slowly, in the deliberate way of a man thinking out a puzzle, Rimbow eased himself off the floor, got to one knee, then hoisted himself upright. He felt dizzy, and sick at his stomach. He was aware of blood's warm wetness on his shoulder, but the lower part of his back didn't feel wet, nor painful when he moved. There was no feeling in it at all. Yet he distinctly remembered the terrific pound of bullets.

19

How could that be? How was it that he could stand up after all that shooting?

"The dirty double-crossing thief!" Tanner whined.

Rimbow peered down at him. "Thief?" he asked dully.

Tanner didn't look at him. The trader's pale, pain-tightened face was tilted down as if the wound beneath his pressing palms fascinated him. "He robbed us both," Tanner muttered. "Me and you—both."

Then Jim Rimbow recalled the gold lining in his leather vest. He didn't need to look to know the vest was gone; he could tell that by the lack of weight. But as some of the numbness receded from his back and a throbbing ache set in, Rimbow understood why those bullets hadn't penetrated his body. The first two had smashed against the tightly packed gold eagles, knocking him over so that the third slug sliced horizontally across his left shoulder as he went down.

Rimbow's lips twisted into a mirthless smile. Fate played peculiar tricks on a man. Senseless damned tricks that were twisty as a sack of snakes. The gold, which had motivated the shooting, had saved his life. Guessing that the bullet which creased his shoulder had gone on to hit Tanner, Rimbow gave a low hoot of amusement. That, by God, was the twistiest trick of all!

"Hell of a time to laugh," Tanner whispered. "Can't you see I'm bleeding to death?"

"Sure," Rimbow said. "And I'm sorry, Jube. Sorry you're going to die."

"Then do something!" Tanner pleaded.

A mocking grin altered Rimbow's whisker-shagged cheeks. He said, "You know why I'm sorry, Jube. Because I'd have liked to do the shooting myself." Then he asked sharply, "Who did it?"

Tanner ignored the question. He kept pressing his hands to his bloody paunch and mumbling and moaning, his glazed eyes set in a hypnotic stare at the dribbling blood which stained his pants.

"Quit your damned groaning and tell me who did the shooting!" Rimbow commanded. "Speak up before I kick your teeth down your yellow throat!"

"It was Worden," Tanner said. "He stopped by here yesterday. Acted like a man who'd take your place, so I propositioned him."

As if fearing Rimbow's displeasure, he whined, "You said it was your last trip—that you was going to quit."

Recalling how this blubbery man had lied to him about the bay horse, Rimbow announced, "And you framed a deal to split my money between you."

Tanner nodded, resentment deepening the ruts on his lardy cheeks. "The double-cros sing bastard took it all. He robbed us both."

Rimbow glanced at the front door, saw how it had been pushed away from the wall, and understood that his assailant had waited there instead of in the back room. He thought, so simple a trick I overlooked it. . . .

Tanner moaned. "My guts are on fire!" For the first time he looked up at Rimbow. "Do something to stop the blood," he pleaded. He gave a long, pain-prodded groan that ended in a sob. "Please do something, Jim."

Tanner's lips were blue, except where a crimson froth stained them, and now his bald head sagged sideways. "I'm bleeding to death," he whispered as if reluctant to share an intimate secret. "I'm going to die."

"Which way did Worden go?" Rimbow asked.

Tanner said wheezily, "North."

Then his head lolled loosely and his blood-smeared hands sagged until they rested palms up on his broad thighs. Sitting so, with an expression of utter resignation on his slack-jawed face, Tanner looked like a man already dead.

Quickly Rimbow demanded, "What does Worden look like?"

Tanner tried to speak again. He coughed and spewed blood and said, "He's—he's—" But the distorted words he mumbled were a meaningless jumble. He let out a long, gurgling sigh, and when it ended, Jube Tanner was dead.

It was an odd thing. There had been no pity in Jim Rimbow for an agony-wracked scoundrel who double-crossed him. Alive, Jube Tanner had seemed wholly hateful—a despicable mass of blubbery flesh, less human than a hog. But now that Tanner was dead his bar-propped body attained a dignity and humanness that had its effect upon Rimbow. Recalling other occasions like this—several of them during the time he had worn a town marshal's badge in Abilene and in the Brazos country before that—Rimbow wondered why this was so. Why did death bestow a mantle of dignity on men like Jube Tanner? How was it that a man could live like a pig, or a wild beast, conniving and killing and despoiling, yet the instant he died acquire this queerly impelling stature?

Shrugging off the spell of it, Rimbow helped himself

to a few staples from the shelves. When he passed Tanner's body on his way to the door he said, "I'd plant you proper, Jube, only I'm in somewhat of a hurry."

Quickly stowing the provisions in his saddlebags, Rimbow mounted and angled across the yard until he picked up the bay's tracks. Then, remembering the penned horses, he doubled back to open the corral gate so they could get to a stack of hay behind the barn.

The bay's tracks were plain enough. Reading sign as he followed them across the stage road and into brush, Rimbow observed that Worden had ridden at a shuffling trot for the first couple miles. After that the bay's hoofprints were deeper and farther spaced, showing that he'd gone into a lope.

It occurred to Rimbow that Worden probably thought he was dead, and wouldn't be expecting pursuit. If that were true there might be a chance of overtaking him before he got to a town. That, he understood, was his only real chance of retrieving his gold-laden vest—to overtake Worden on the trail. For even though he had seen the bay horse, he hadn't observed its brand, and might fail to identify it among other horses. There were a hell-smear of bays in Arizona Territory.

A little before sundown Rimbow lost the tracks on a bald ridge of shelving slab rock. Dismounting, he led his tired horse in a circle that revealed no sign of recent travel. Worden had been headed north when the bay's hoofprints petered out, but that didn't mean he would continue in that direction. The dry-gulcher might deliberately have left a plain trail to establish the fact

he had ridden northward, after which he could have
sneaked off in some other direction.

Patiently Rimbow made another circle, scanning the
rock that was like smelter slag, so hard that shod hoofs
wouldn't scar it. Then he put his eyes to a questing
study of the broken, brush-blotched country ahead,
hoping for sight of a dust plume. He found none. To
the northwest the Dragoons rose in rugged splendor,
their eastern slopes already cloaked in lavender shadows.
Worden, Rimbow guessed, was no more than one hour's
riding time ahead—but in what direction?

What did he look like? What was his first name?

Rimbow put his mind to dredging up names and
faces out of the past, trying to decide if he had ever
met a man by the name of Worden. Not in the Seventh
Cavalry, as far as he could recall, nor afterward during
his stay in Abilene. Tanner had said that Worden
looked like a man who'd take a gun-running job. Probably a tough drifter, or a gunslinger on the dodge. Rimbow had met plenty of that breed in Texas. Remembering the night Mike O'Mara had saved his bacon, Rimbow
thought he had almost met one too many, but none
named Worden. And there'd been nobody by that name
in Apache Basin.

Some damned saddle tramp, Rimbow decided.

With the fatalistic gesture of a losing gambler, Rimbow shrugged, and then winced. His shirt, which had
pulled free of the blood-gummed wound when he dismounted, had stuck again to his flesh.

For the first time the enormity of Tanner's double-
cross came to Rimbow. Instead of returning to Reserva-

tion with sixteen hundred dollars, he would arrive flat broke. Not a dollar to show for risking his hide below the border. Instead of paying off the bank loan and having some money left besides, he would have to tell Mike that he had failed, and his failure meant they could not go on with the ranch.

Thinking of the two men who had conspired to do this to him, Rimbow swore savagely, then mounted and rode down the first canyon he came to and, finding a shallow seep of water, decided to camp for the night. There was no hurry, now that he had lost Worden's trail. Tomorrow he would ride a wider circle, but even if he picked up the bay's tracks and followed them to some town he would have little chance of identifying Worden. And there was no hurry about getting back to Reservation. None at all. Instead of being eager to reach home, Rimbow dreaded arriving there broke. Not that Mike O'Mara would blame him. The Irishman would probably fun him about it, for that was Mike's way. Money didn't mean much to Mike O'Mara since he'd got over the idea of marrying a girl named Eve Chastain. Rimbow frowned, thinking of that affair. When it was over, Mike had gone on a wild drinking spree in town— so wild that Sheriff Weaver had finally locked him in a jail cell.

Women, Rimbow thought disgustedly. It was a hell of a thing how much trouble a sweet-smelling female could cause. His own mother had deserted a hard-working husband and her ten-year-old son to traipse off with a guitar-playing drifter. The blight of that abandonment had turned his father into a drunkard who finally lost his life in a fight over a town trollop a sober man wouldn't have shared a blanket with in a blizzard.

Rimbow hobbled his horse and gathered firewood. It got cold in this high country after sundown, and he missed the protection of his old leather vest. The proprietor of a saddle shop in Abilene had given it to him as a token of appreciation for disarming a boozy Texan who'd threatened the old man's life. Rimbow smiled, recalling the merchant's words: "This is poor pay for what you done." But it had turned out to be good pay. It had saved his life.

He built his fire, prepared his frugal supper and ate it without relish. The wound in his shoulder hurt and his back ached as if it had been pounded with a fence post. Like a man deliberately tormenting himself, Rimbow recalled the last time he had seen Mike O'Mara.

"I'll be back with more money than you can shake a stick at," he had promised.

Mike wanted to come with him, but Rimbow had vetoed the offer, insisting that someone must take care of the ranch. And just before riding off he had warned Mike about keeping out of trouble. "Don't mix into the Chastain-Jardine rumpus," he cautioned. "Let them battle it out between themselves."

That was one of the things which had caused Eve Chastain to turn her back on Mike. She had wanted him to quit a poverty-striken cow camp and take a job as foreman on her father's Spade ranch. But Mike had his pride, and he'd said no—he'd wanted to be his own man and not beholden to her father for his wages.

Rimbow cursed, thinking that Mike wouldn't be his own man much longer. If the bank foreclosed they'd have to find jobs on some bigger outfit. "Working for wages," Rimbow muttered, and cursed again. He and Mike had soldiered together in the Seventh Cavalry. But their real friendship had begun in Abilene one night when a reckless Irishman had sided a town marshal who'd got himself into a tight. Afterward, when Rimbow quit the law job, they had come to Arizona and built themselves the beginnings of a cow outfit.

Rimbow made a cigarette and smoked it. He was sitting like that, frowning in deep introspection, when a gruff voiced called from beyond the rim of his firelight, "Hoist 'em, feller!"

For a fleeting instant Rimbow weighed his chances. He made a plain target, outlined against the fireglow—a target no marksman would miss—yet he teetered on the thin edge of decision, toying with the thought of diving across the glowing embers.

"Make up your mind," the voice prompted, and Rimbow guessed its owner was less than fifteen feet away.

"All right, Worden," Rimbow said and raised his hands. Turning, he watched a tall, hawk-featured man step warily into the circle of firelight—a man he recognized instantly.

A slow grin eased Rimbow's lips as he asked, "Some off your home range, aren't you, Hawk?"

Marshal Halliday eyed him narrowly, holding his gun hip high. "I could say the same for you," he suggested, and lifted Rimbow's Colt from holster, using his left hand to accomplish the chore with expert swiftness.

Then he said, "Seems careless of a man to sit dreaming at a campfire only ten or twelve miles from the man he murdered. Where's your pardner at?"

"Pardner?"

"The name you called sounded like Worden," Halliday said. "You must have been expecting him."

"Not exactly. But I was hoping to see him some time soon."

Halliday's tight eyes continued to study him. "Didn't the two of you leave Tanner's place together?"

"No. About an hour apart, I think. You don't happen to know Worden, do you, Hawk?"

"What's he look like?"

"Well, that depends," Rimbow said dryly, and gave his attention to rolling a cigarette. "If he happened to get shot between the eyes he'd look like a corpse, which is how I'd like to see him. Otherwise he would look about the same as the last time you saw him."

"I never saw a man named Worden," the marshal said.

"Me neither," Rimbow admitted.

Hawk peered at him in the baffled way of a man not sure what he was seeing. "You drunk?" he demanded.

Rimbow shook his head. "Wish I was, though. Drunk and dreaming." He motioned to the smoke-blackened coffee can and said, "Have yourself some Arbuckle."

Watching Halliday pour the coffee, Rimbow wondered what had brought him so far from his Oklahoma head-quarters. Hawk had made a name for himself in the Strip country. A big name. Why had he shown up at Jube Tanner's store the same day a gun-runner returned from Sonora? It could be too tight a fit for coincidence, Rimbow thought. U. S. Deputy Marshals weren't in the habit of taking pleasure trips. They usually had a reason when they traveled. Especially Hawk Halliday.

Had the bleachy-eyed old lawdog come looking for a border-jumper? The thought put a chill in Rimbow. It caused him to hunker down on his heels, close to the fire.

Halliday followed suit, and for a small interval they sat in silence with the fire between them. More than the fire, though, separated them—almost five years. There had been a time when they were both on the same side of the law fence—the badge side. But not now. Six trips into Sonora with gun-laden mules made the difference.

Somewhere up the canyon a coyote let go its yammering, two-toned howl. After that there was only the sound of Rimbow's horse browsing in the nearby darkness.

Finally Halliday asked, "Why did you shoot Tanner?"

"I didn't."

Halliday finished his coffee and took out a pipe. He seemed wholly relaxed as he filled it from a pouch and then lit it with a burning twig, but Rimbow observed that Hawk's right hand was never more than twelve inches from his gun.

"You left a pretty plain trail," Halliday suggested.

"So did Worden, for a ways."

"Did he kill Tanner?"

Rimbow nodded. "It's quite a story, Hawk. And one you might not believe. But I'll tell it, regardless."

Presently, when he had described the shooting at Tanner's place without mentioning his gold-laden vest,

29

Halliday asked, "How come Worden only shot you once —and that just a crease?"

It was a question Rimbow didn't choose to answer truthfully. Better, he thought, to be suspected of murder than admit being a gun-runner. "Maybe Worden thought he drilled me first shot, and then turned his gun on Tanner."

There was no visible alteration in Halliday's expression. His fire-lit face revealed neither acceptance nor rejection. Eager to convince the lawman, Rimbow said, "Worden was set on robbing Tanner, and I happened to get in his way."

"It don't tally," Hawk said.

"Why not?"

"Well, for one thing, there were four empty shells. Not two." His voice went sharp as he demanded, "If those shots didn't come from your gun why did you lie about them?"

Rimbow shrugged. This was no ordinary badge-toter he was trying to convince with half truths—no tin-star politician to be bamboozled by jawbone trickery. This was the one they called The Hawk.

Looking Halliday in the eye he said quietly, "I didn't kill Tanner. Can't you see I'm telling the truth?"

"No," Halliday muttered.

"What makes you think I'm lying?"

"Well, you left Jube Tanner sitting there against his bar. You didn't even shut the door to keep varmints away from his body."

"I was in a big rush to trail Worden," Rimbow explained doggedly.

"Then why'd you take time to turn Tanner's horses out of the corral?"

"So they wouldn't miss their supper."

"I suppose you liked those horses better than Tanner," Halliday suggested.

"Never said I liked Tanner. In fact I hated his greedy guts."

A knowing smile slanted Halliday's gaunt cheeks. "That's what I figured," he said, and drew a pair of handcuffs from his coat pocket.

"I tell you I didn't shoot him," Rimbow insisted, and understood that Halliday thought he had trapped him and had made up his mind—that nothing he could say now would alter this lawman's belief that he had murdered Jube Tanner.

"That's for a jury to decide," Hawk said. "I'll turn you over to Sheriff Weaver in Reservation."

Rimbow cursed. He stood there in the dismal fashion of a man who knew he was beaten, his face showing a solemn resignation. But as Halliday reached out to manacle his wrists, Rimbow's right hand clamped into a fist that lifted in a vicious uppercut. It caught Halliday under the chin and knocked him back so abruptly that Rimbow missed with his left.

Rimbow pitched forward, hitting Halliday with a sledging right to the belly that made the lawman loose an agonized grunt. Halliday floundered sideways, and slashed at Rimbow's head with the handcuffs.

The impact of metal against his temple was like an explosion. Rimbow made one final attempt to grasp Halliday's gun and, missing, fell headlong. When his

31

senses cleared he saw the lawman standing above him.

Rimbow sat up. He shook his head, attempting to dispel the oppressive lethargy that gripped him. He lifted his shackled hands to his forehead, felt the blood there, and cursed morosely.

"Your own damned fault," Halliday muttered. He examined the wound above Rimbow's right eye and predicted, "You'll live." Hunkering on his heels by the fire, Halliday added: "To be hung."

3

Ride—or Die

DAYLIGHT was coming when Rimbow was awakened by Halliday's announcement, "Coffee's hot."

Hawk unlocked the handcuffs and stepped quickly back. He had saddled his horse, which Rimbow recognized as Tanner's dun gelding. And the saddle was Jube's centerfire. He was wondering about that while he ate in moody silence. Halliday must have been traveling by stage and then changed his plans to trail Tanner's killer.

"How you feel?" the marshal asked.

Rimbow shrugged. He poured his coffee, asked, "Were you heading toward Tombstone by stage?"

"Reservation."

....*Then he hasn't come looking for a gun-runner,* Rimbow thought. But you couldn't tell about a man like Hawk. The old lawdog might be playing it foxy, might know he'd caught his gun-runner and was waiting to see how the murder charge made out.

Presently, as Rimbow saddled the sorrel gelding, he wondered if Halliday would dispense with the handcuffs, now that it was daylight. It wouldn't be quite so

33

bad riding into Reservation free-handed—at least folks wouldn't know he was under arrest until afterward. But that hope was soon dispelled, for the lawman manacled his wrists, saying, "Just so you don't get any more damned fool notions."

Rimbow glanced at his empty holster. "Don't take any chances, do you, Hawk?"

"Not with killers." As they rode on up the canyon Hawk added: "I've heard you didn't take too many chances when you were wearing the badge in Abilene. They say you shot first, and did your talking afterward."

Rimbow frowned, resenting the reputation that had been given him by loud-mouthed gossips. "You should know how it was with me," he muttered. "That was a tough town. A man with a star on his vest was a free target. But folks never thought about that." Then he asked, "What you doing in this country?"

"Well, I'm looking for a couple fugitives that are wanted for robbing the U. S. mail in Texas. Got word from Sam Chastain that I might find them riding for Jardine's Circle J outfit, which is giving Sam a fight for the graze."

"So it's finally turned into a shooting ruckus," Rimbow mused, and hoped that Mike had kept clear of it.

For a time, then, they rode in silence, climbing long slopes where the barbed branches of catclaw and mesquite snatched at Rimbow's shirt sleeves as he held his manacled hands up to protect his face. Rimbow scanned the dusty trail for sign of recent hoofprints, and finding none, guessed that Worden had headed toward Tombstone. He was tempted to tell Halliday about the double-eagles, and admit how he had come by them; to suggest they go to Tombstone and try to catch Worden. But he discarded the impulse, knowing that if the lawman believed his story, Hawk would have him on a federal offense. Even if Worden were caught there'd be only the word of a confessed gun-runner against him. And that might not be enough to convict him. Better, Rimbow decided, to take his chances with a jury trial, or hope for an opportunity to escape.

But the injustice of it griped his soul. For the first time in his life he had made some big money—fast money. Sure, it had been a shady deal. The export law of one country had been broken, and the import law of another. But there'd been no theft involved, no real crookedness. Just a matter of pitting his wits and risking his hide against the chance to save a debt-ridden ranch. He had won his gamble, too, and quit when he had enough. Yet he had failed because of a man he'd never seen.

The trail dipped occasionally into dry washes and circled through rock-studded hills, with the brush giving way to wind-twisted scrub oak and occasional stands of pine. At midafternoon they crossed the crest of Durango Divide and began a switch-back descent of its north slope.

Later, as they crossed a broad meadow, Halliday said, "Spade's old horse pasture."

"Not any more," Rimbow told him. "Jardine is using it. He has crowded Chastain off this graze."

"How come?" Hawk inquired.

Rimbow shrugged, not interested in explaining Apache

Basin's troubles. He rode in moody silence now, dreading the ordeal of appearing handcuffed on Reservation's Main Street. A penniless man could hold his head high if he chose. A shabby saddle tramp could retain the tattered remnants of his pride. But not a prisoner with manacled wrists. There was something wholly degrading about handcuffs; they made a man feel like an animal. And that's how he would feel in a jail cell. Like a coyote in a cage.

Rimbow cursed, sensing how it would be, with folks gawking at him on Main Street. He turned to Halliday and asked, "How about taking these things off me for the ride into town. I'll give you my word not to make a break."

Halliday seemed surprised. He asked, "What difference does it make, one way or the other?"

"Handcuffs make a man feel like a freak."

Halliday chuckled. He asked, "You ever think about that when you wore a badge?"

"No. But I'm thinking about it now."

"Well, you can't keep a murder charge secret. Everybody in town will know about it soon enough."

Rimbow glanced at his shackled wrists. "It's hard to explain. But I'd like to be shut of them, Hawk."

They were riding through a narrow pass between two timbered ridges now. Halliday seemed to be considering Rimbow's request—he said finally, "Well, if it means that much—"

At this moment a bullet whanged past Rimbow's head, its sound instantly followed by a rifle's report. Dodging instinctively, he yanked his horse into a pivoting turn.

He felt the air lash of a slug that missed his right cheek by a feather-fine margin, and heard Halliday blurt a curse. The lawman was also whirling his horse in an attempt to turn back. Rimbow saw him tilt up his gun. But Halliday didn't fire; he collapsed as if struck by an invisible club. His body sagged off to one side, spooking the excited dun. When the horse wheeled sharply, Hawk went down in a limp headlong fall.

A bullet ricocheted off rock beside Rimbow, and in the next moment of dust-hazed confusion, his horse collapsed, dropping so abruptly that Rimbow had no time to jump clear.

He lay motionless, his right leg pinned beneath the dead sorrel's side. In the sudden hush he heard a rider moving somewhere on the ridge behind him and wondered if the dry-gulcher was Worden.

A dislodged stone clattered into the pass. Rimbow held himself rigidly still, not daring to turn his head to look up there. It occurred to him that it probably wasn't Worden. The latter would be bellied up to a bar by now, or spending his stolen gold on some sweet-smelling bawd. More likely, the dry-gulcher was one of Jardine's toughs who had glimpsed the silver star on Halliday's vest. One of the renegades who had reason for stopping a U. S. Marshal on the prowl.

A green-bellied horsefly lit on Rimbow's cheek, its contact causing a reflex twitch that Rimbow barely controlled. The rider on the ridge was taking his time, probably waiting to see if there was sign of life down here, and itching for an excuse to do some more shooting. Another fly lit on Rimbow's nose, flittered up to his forehead and perched on the raw gash there. Rimbow kept his face muscles steady, not sure whether the man above him was high enough to see his face. But he could probably see that the sorrel had him pinned down.

It seemed like a long time before Rimbow heard hoofs tromp above him, and then, for a tight moment, he wasn't sure whether the dry-gulcher was riding toward him, or away—until the sound faded out completely.

He let loose a gusty sigh—he was a fool for luck.

But presently, when he tried to pull free of the dead sorrel, he wasn't so sure his luck would hold. There didn't seem to be a great deal of weight on his leg—he eased around and managed to sit up—but he couldn't pull free.

Hawk Halliday sprawled where he had fallen. Blood showed on the lawman's scalp. He had lost his hat and there was a red stain on his gray hair. His pants leg was sogged with blood where a bullet had ripped into his thigh, and Rimbow thought with a sudden chill, *Got it twice. . . .*

Bracing his free boot against the saddle, he put all his strength into a struggle to extricate himself. For a moment, as the trapped leg seemed to loosen, he believed he was going to make it. But his spur had become fouled in the cinch webbing; the leg could come only so far, and there wasn't enough leeway to work the rowel free. He struggled with the desperation of a trapped animal, until exhaustion forced him to quit— to lay back, panting and sweating.

Resting, he watched a buzzard circle slowly overhead. How was it, he wondered, that carrion birds never failed to arrive at the scene of death? What fantastic sense of sight or smell attracted them with such unerring accuracy? He understood that it was the dead sorrel the scavenger was after, but the bird's patient circling gave his thoughts a morbid turn. A man could starve to death on this little-used trail—trapped as he was, he could die for lack of food and water.

Rimbow hadn't heard the man ride up behind him—didn't know he was there until a voice asked, "You stuck?"

He tensed, not turning to look, scarcely breathing. For a dozen heartbeats he waited. Finally he said, "Yes."

"Leg broke?"

Rimbow shook his head.

There was another moment of silence. The temptation to turn and look was strong in Rimbow, but he understood that there was nothing to be gained by looking into the muzzle of a gun. For that was what he would see. There'd be a hand holding the gun, and an arm connected to the hand—and a face. The last thought made him wary.

"Ain't you curious to see who done the shooting?" the man asked.

Rimbow shook his head.

"You hurt?"

Rimbow shook his head again.

There was another silence. Then the man asked, "What's the charge ag'in' you?"

"Murder."

As if finding some magic key in the word, the man said, "Then I done you a good turn, killing the lawdog." It was not a question.

"Suppose," Rimbow agreed.

"Reckon you wouldn't do no talkin' if I turned you loose from that pony," the man suggested.

Rimbow shook his head. In the ensuing moment of silence an ember of hope flared into flame in him. The handcuffs he'd wanted so urgently to be free of might make the difference here. . . .

He heard the slight creak of saddle leather as the man dismounted. The other came around him and bent down to untie the saddle's latigo—a medium-sized man wearing a battered, flat-crowned hat, a calico shirt and new batwing chaps. Looking at him now, Rimbow knew instantly that he had never seen this face before. Yet he had seen a hundred faces like it—heavy, blank-eyed, ingrained with viciousness and impassive brutality.

As the stranger undid the latigo loops, Rimbow glanced at Halliday's sprawled form and wondered if Hawk was still breathing. If he happened to groan, he would be dead as a gutted steer in the time it took the stranger to trigger one well-aimed shot.

"You're loose," the man announced.

Rimbow pulled his boot free of the sorrel's weight. He said, "Much obliged," and got up. Returning circulation needled the leg with prickling darts as he stepped over to Halliday and used both hands to pluck the tubular handcuff key from Hawk's vest pocket.

The stranger watched him maneuver the key into the locking mechanism and asked, "Want a riding job?"

40

Rimbow flung the handcuffs as far as he could throw them. "Who with?"

"Riley Jardine's outfit."

In the moment while Rimbow considered that, the man said slyly, "Good wages, and not much work."

"Gun wages?"

The stranger nodded. A smile rutted his sun-blackened cheeks as he said, "Some good boys to ride with. Texas boys."

But the smile didn't reach his eyes, and now he canted his head, listening with the feral intensity of an animal. "Somebody coming," he said and went quickly to his horse. "The lawdog's pony is in that brush behind you." He rode carefully up the north slope.

Rimbow nodded and started for the thicket, but paused to pick up the pistol that lay near Halliday's body. The sound of the approaching rider was clearer now, but Rimbow kept to a walk as he neared the grazing dun, hoping that Tanner's horse wouldn't spook. As he reached for the dangling reins, the animal greeted the oncoming rider with a whinny.

"Whoa, boy—stand!" Rimbow commanded.

The dun stopped and Rimbow grabbed the reins. A rider broke through brush a scant dozen yards away, one Rimbow recognized instantly—Eve Chastain.

She saw him and reined in, flushing. "Jim Rimbow!" And then, as if feeling the need to explain her presence on the disputed range: "I saw buzzards circling and came to see what attracted them."

She was as goldenly beautiful as ever, but the sight of her aroused only a bitterness in Rimbow. He mo-

41

tioned toward the dead sorrel, wondering if Jardine's gunslinger was near enough to hear this talk, and hoping he wasn't. "We got dry-gulched."

"We?"

"Hawk Halliday was riding with me."

The announcement had an instant effect upon Eve Chastain. "Oh mercy! Is Hawk hurt?"

Rimbow held up a palm. "Keep your voice down. There's a man up there—a man with a gun."

"But is Hawk hurt?" she demanded.

Rimbow nodded. Thinking of the stranger who might be watching this, he said, "If Halliday is still alive he should be toted out of here in a wagon. You'd better ride to the ranch and get one."

"I'm going to look at him," she insisted and went on past Rimbow. He watched her dismount and kneel beside Halliday, heard her say, "Poor Uncle Jeff!" Then she turned and as if commanding one of her father's cowboys, called, "Go get a wagon—and hurry!"

His old resentment flaring up in him, Rimbow said rankly, "Get out of here before you get hurt."

She looked at him, animosity tightening the soft oval of her face. "I'm staying with Jeff. Don't stand there and argue. Do as you're told."

Rimbow shrugged and thought to hell with it . . . what happened from here on out didn't concern him. Chances were the stranger wouldn't shoot a woman, or come close enough for her to see him. But presently, as he rode through the pass, it occurred to him that what happened to Halliday concerned him aplenty. If Hawk died, a murder charge would die with him. He wondered, *Why am I hurrying?* Yet he kept the dun to a strong, steady lope.

He peered over his shoulder, wondering if the beefy-faced gunman would try to overtake him—and it came to him that if the Jardine rider hadn't freed him from the dead sorrel he would have been found by Eve Chastain, trapped and handcuffed. The man had done him a double favor for a fact.

There was no sign of travel on the ridge which now sloped off gradually to a broad bench where Spade's headquarters lay. Looking at the distant sprawl of corrals and sheds flanking the adobe house, Rimbow compared it with the cow camp in the Hoot Owl Hills— the homestead he and Mike would probably lose.

He was approaching Spade's horse trap a mile west of the ranch yard when a rider came out to meet him, a gray-haired oldster who squinted his eyes against afternoon's slanting sunlight and said, "So it's you—" as if he'd been expecting someone of importance, and Jim Rimbow didn't matter, one way or the other.

He was a proud one, this Sam Chastain. You could tell that by the way he sat a horse, straight as a buggy-whip, and the way he held his head. His down-swirling mustache and Vandyke beard gave him the look of a Southern aristocrat. Guessing that Chastain's hair had once been blond, Rimbow thought, *Like Eve's* . . . and they shared the same arrogance. Riley Jardine had shrunk the size of Chastain's range, but he hadn't shriveled the old man's pride.

"Did you see my daughter?" Chastain inquired.

Rimbow nodded. "She's up there in the pass trail with

Hawk Halliday. He's bad hurt, and needs a wagon."

"What happened?" Chastain demanded.

"Somebody dry-gulched us."

"God A'mighty!" Chastain exclaimed. He shook his head, and said sharply, "Hurry, man—go get the wagon."

He started to ride past but Rimbow said, "Get it yourself."

Chastain pulled up. For an instant he seemed astonished, as if he couldn't comprehend a man refusing to obey him. In this brief interval Rimbow saw an odd bafflement cross the old man's high-beaked face. Then the other whirled his horse and spurred it into a run.

Quartering south of the yard, Rimbow felt a continuing resentment. Who the hell did these Chastains think they were—you'd think, by God, that he owed them money. Or was on Spade's payroll.

Mike would get a chuckle out of this when he heard about it. Thinking of the reunion with his partner, Rimbow felt an increasing eagerness to get home. Even though he was returning empty-handed it would be good to see the Hoot Owls again, to eat at his own table and sleep in his own bed—until a bank took the place over. He thought, *I'll get a bottle, regardless.* . . .

When he came to the stage road, Rimbow glanced back and saw a wagon going toward the pass. A rider came from the front gate at a gallop. Moments later, Felipe Chacon, Spade's Mexican horse wrangler, passed him without slowing down.

"I go for fetch Doctor Carter!" Felipe shouted.

Watching the other hightail on down the road, it occurred to Rimbow that he could have delayed this deal by not telling Chastain about the marshal—that an hour or two might have made the difference between Halliday's living or dying.

For there was no wondering what would happen if Halliday survived. He would hunt down a man he considered guilty of murder.

4

While Bullets Wait

RIMBOW CAME to the dugway above Reservation a little before sundown. Seeing how the place had grown, he said, "Boomtown," smearing the word with contempt. There had been no tents or canvas-sided shacks in Reservation four months ago. Now, by the look of it, there were a hundred or more, cramming every vacant lot on Main Street and along Burro Alley.

Smoke from a switch engine tainted the air as he rode down the dugway. Telegraph poles flanked twin ribbons of steel across the eastward desert. Four months ago this had been a cowtown dozing in the sun, just a wide place in the stage road. There'd been one saloon, Poetry Pete Eggleston's Alhambra, and a bar at the Palace Hotel. Now, Rimbow supposed, there were half a dozen dives. Contemplating the dust-hazed town, he remembered Abilene with its gamblers and fancy women and land speculators—all the riffraff that invariably followed the westward thrust of railroad construction. Booze and bawds and bunco artists—that was what progress brought to a country, he thought with cynical amusement. Well, it was no meat off his back, one way or the other. Reservation's so-called progress wouldn't reach to the Hoot Owls, which was where he and Mike spent most of their time.

Main Street's wheel-rutted dust was swirled by all manner of conveyance. A jerkline freighter cursed his eight-horse hitch into making a turn for the wagonyard behind Martin's Mercantile; two ore wagons, returning empty to the Silver King mine, northwest of town, rumbled along Burro Alley; ranch rigs and saddled horses lined hitchracks along both sides of the street and pedestrians tromped the plank walks.

Scanning the signs above the sidewalk, he saw one that startled him. Huge, red-lettered, it announced: THE LADY GAY SALOON—LEW TIFFANY, PROPRIETOR. There had been a Lady Gay Saloon on the south side of the Kansas Pacific tracks in Abilene, complete with slick-fingered cardsharks and sweet-smelling percentage girls. Recalling his last visit there, Rimbow felt an odd sense of foreboding. Except for Mike O'Mara he wouldn't have left that other Lady Gay alive. Mike had made the difference that night. . . .

Rimbow was dismounting at the Alhambra hitchrack when Doc Carter's red-wheeled rig went past, with Felipe sharing the seat and his horse tied behind. The medico had his bay pacer going at a fast clip. Watching the bay's precise and seemingly effortless motion, Rimbow guessed that Doc would keep him at it all the way to Spade. And if anyone could save Hawk Halliday, Doc Carter could. There wasn't a better gunshot specialist in Arizona Territory.

Going on into the saloon, Rimbow found it deserted

except for the old man who stood with his big belly propped on the bar's beveled edge. "Where's all your customers at?" Rimbow asked.

"The Lady Gay, and them girl dives," Poetry Pete Eggleston said. "You just ride in?"

Rimbow nodded. He peered at the solemn-faced saloonman and said censuringly, "A man stays gone four long months. He dreams about the big welcome he'll get at his favorite bar, and then what happens? Not so much as the offer of a drink on the house."

A trace of humor altered Eggleston's moon face, but his eyes retained their gravity, and now he said, "You're three days too late."

"Late? For what?"

Eggleston reached for his private bottle of bourbon and poured a generous drink. He said soberly, "For Mike O'Mara's funeral," and handed Rimbow the brimming glass.

Jim Rimbow took the drink and held it rigidly poised. He peered at Eggleston for a long moment before asking, "You mean Mike is dead?"

The saloonman nodded.

Rimbow stared at the glass in his hand, not seeing the bourbon's amber glow or savoring its aroma.

"Drink it down," Eggleston suggested.

Rimbow paid him no heed. As if repeating a thing he couldn't comprehend, he said quietly, "Mike is dead." He gave the glass a continuing appraisal and said it again. "Mike is dead."

"I closed my place for the funeral," Eggleston said. "The preacher quoted Thomas Gray's glorious *Epitaph*

48

for the final benediction. Would you like to hear it?"

Rimbow shrugged, whereupon Poetry Pete spoke the lines with a solemn fervor:

> *"Here rests his head upon the lap of Earth,*
> *A youth to Fortune and to Fame unknown. . . .*
> *He gave to Misery, all he had, a tear;*
> *He gained from Heaven, 'twas all he wished,*
> *a friend!"*

Rimbow took his drink at a gulp. He asked, "Who killed him, Pete?"

"Lew Tiffany. He runs the Lady Gay Saloon. They say it was a fair enough fight, except that Mike was drunk."

Rimbow cursed. He said rankly, "You mean fair enough to satisfy Sheriff Pinky Weaver." Then, in the whispering tone of a man dredging deep and despising what he found, Rimbow said, "Abilene." The past had a way of catching up with a man sooner or later, no matter how far he rode.

Presently he asked, "How'd it happen?"

"It started over a woman," Poetry Pete said. "The best looking female that ever swung a bustle around here. You've never seen one like her, Jim. She's what Swinburnesaw in Dolores McCord when he wrote about fierce midnights and famishing morrows, all the joys of the flesh, all the sorrows."

There had been a time when Jim Rimbow enjoyed Poetry Pete's incongruous affectations. He didn't now. "Give it to me straight," he suggested.

"Well, I'm trying to put it so you'll understand what

49

prodded Mike O'Mara to such seeming foolishness," Poetry Pete explained. "If you know Marlene you'll know why he fell in love with her."

"Love, hell!" Rimbrow scoffed. "With a saloon hustler?"

"Marlene is no wanton hussy practicing casual revealment or teasing trickery," Poetry Pete insisted.

"I don't care what she is, Pete. By God, are you going to tell me what happened?"

Eggleston poured him another drink. He said soothingly, "I'm giving you time to cool down, Jim. There's no use of going off half-cocked and maybe getting yourself killed. It was a bad thing, Mike dying like he did. But you can't blame Tiffany for all of it. And you can't blame Marlene. She's a fine, gracious young woman if I ever saw one. Supports her crippled husband by singing songs at the Lady Gay. She's the living image of a man's campfire dreams. She's warmth against the cold and a banquet to satisfy his hidden hungers."

"It sounds as if you're the one Tiffany should have shot," Rimbow muttered derisively.

Eggleston smiled at him. "If I was ten, fifteen years younger he might've had reason to shoot me. You'll understand when you see her, Jim. You'll know why half the miners from the Silver King come to town every night just to hear her sing. You'd think every day was Saturday the way the cowpunchers ride in. Not just the young ones, but old broken-down mossyhorns. They come all the way from Broken Bit, and Gaviota Pass. Even nesters, with wives at home, drive their beat-up wagons to town for a look at Marlene."

Frowning in the fashion of a patient man forced

to wait for what he wanted, Rimbow said, "So Mike fell for a saloon singer. Then what?"

"Well, he just couldn't stay away from her, Jim. The first night he came in here sad-eyed as a hound dog because she refused to let him walk home with her after work. He hadn't noticed she was wearing a wedding ring. He'd just told her he wanted to marry her, and wouldn't take no for an answer. You understand how Mike was. Impetuous, and a romantic Mick into the bargain. Well, Marlene held up her ringed finger for him to see and said he was a trifle late with his proposal." Pete paused, then went on: "Mike was two thirds drunk when he talked to me. But he had one thing straight in his mind—a profound conviction that I adhered to in my youth, and still do, with certain reservations."

Tension was mounting almost unbearably in Rimbow. "Tell me the facts, Pete—the facts."

"In my own way," Eggleston said blandly, and poured himself a drink. "Mike understood that a full-blooded man needs a real female woman. With ordinary men it doesn't make much difference, just so they've got somebody to put food on the table and darn their socks of an evening. But for a full-blooded man it's not enough just to have a wife. He needs a woman who wants him—a woman who makes him want her." Eggleston took his drink and smacked his lips. "Even knowing she was married didn't keep Mike away from her. Just being near her seemed to make him feel high as a windmill. He played table stake poker and bought drinks for the house. He tossed silver dollars around as if they were plugged pesos."

51

"How could he do that?" Rimbow demanded. "Where would Mike get the money?"

"Don't know where, but he got it. Bought trinkets for Marlene and kept trying to talk her into letting him walk her home after work. But Lew Tiffany did that pleasant chore himself, saying he wanted no hard feelings among the cash customers. No favorites. And that suited Marlene. She treats them all alike. She sings their favorite songs, and sometimes dances with a man if she likes his looks. I don't know what Tiffany is paying her, but she has turned his place into a gold mine."

"Sure, sure," Rimbow urged. "Now tell me what happened."

"Well, the third night, while Mike was dancing with Marlene, he kissed her. Not just a stolen kiss, you understand, but the real thing. Like a hungry man with a heaping dish. Marlene didn't do a thing. Just waited until he got through and then walked off the floor, not saying a word to anybody. But Lew Tiffany had seen it. He ordered Mike out of the place. Mike laughed at him, and said something about it being the second time Tiffany had tried to spook him. Then he went for his gun."

"And?" Rimbow prompted.

"Well, they say Tiffany put two slugs into him before Mike could raise his gun."

In the moment while Rimbow absorbed the bitter taste of it, Eggleston added, "I'm glad Mike got to kiss her before he died."

One part of the long recital stuck in Rimbow's mind. The part about Mike saying it was the second time

Tiffany had tried to spook him. The memory of that other time was strong in Rimbow now.

Eggleston asked, "Do you know Lew Tiffany?"

Rimbrow nodded.

"Then you know his draw is faster than the flick of a toad's tongue."

Rimbrow ignored that. He lifted the second drink and grimaced as he drank it.

"You heard about the Chastain-Jardine trouble?" Eggleston asked, as if eager to keep up the conversation.

Rimbrow nodded and walked to the doorway.

"You going to call on Tiffany?" the saloonman asked.

"Yes, and when I finish with him I'm going to slap that woman's face."

"Wait, Jim! You lay a hand on Marlene and you'll get lynched!"

Rimbow was untying the dun's reins at the hitchrack when Eggleston's big paunch pushed the batwing gates open. "Mind what I say," the saloonman warned. "Don't take your spite out on Marlene."

Late sunlight slanted into the wide doorway of Monk Finucane's Livery where Rimbow left his horse. The ape-faced Irishman said indignantly, " 'Tis a stinkin' shame what that spalpeen Tiffany done to Mike, and him merely stealin' a kiss the colleen could well afford. Be ye goin' to revenge him, Jim?"

Rimbow nodded and walked on along the street. His eyes registered the fact that there were three new buildings on the south side of Main Street, and two more under construction. The resin smell of green lumber came to his nostrils and the sounds of traffic to his ears. But stronger than any of this was the overwhelming realization that Mike O'Mara was dead. Mike, who'd been so full of life and the joy of living it. So full-blooded, as Eggleston called it. . . .

Dying sunlight fashioned slatted shadows in the corral beyond Finucane's barn; it gilded the Bon Ton Millinery window where two bosomy percentage girls stood contemplating satin finery for sale.

Rimbow's tall, lean-shanked shape cast a long shadow as he strode methodically toward the red-lettered sign that said: LADY GAY SALOON. There was a brittleness in his bleached blue eyes and a kind of controlled savagery in his movements, but with the awful need for vengeance prodding him, his face held no hint of the tension in him.

One of the percentage girls in front of the Bon Ton turned to glance at Rimbow. She smiled, liking what she saw, and when Rimbow revealed no awareness of the invitation of her eyes, she said to the other girl, "He didn't seem to see me at all. He looked at me, but he didn't see me."

"Must be blind," her companion suggested.

Rimbow heard that, and compared this town with Abilene where the fancy women had stayed in their place, across the tracks in Texas Town with the rest of the riffraff. But here they plied their ancient trade on Main Street. He cursed, thinking that Mike had spent his last few days on earth like a parlor-house sport on a spree. And where, he wondered, had Mike got the cash to squander?

Fritz Elmendorf stood in the doorway of his saddle

shop. He said, "Don't look for trouble, Jim. This town is full of it."

"So am I," Rimbow muttered, and presently came abreast of the Mercantile stoop where John Martin stood with Riley Jardine.

"I'm sorry about Mike," the merchant-mayor said. "The Citizens' Committee met last night, and we are going to take definite action."

Rimbow was tempted to ask, *To resurrect Mike?* But because this meek-eyed merchant had been generous with credit to both himself and Mike, he said, "I hear Pinky Weaver said it was a fair fight."

Martin nodded. "Pinky says that about all of them. But something has to be done. The town has grown too big, too fast."

Riley Jardine chuckled. He said, "It will shrink back to normal when the railroad construction crews move on. No sense getting all stirred up about a temporary thing."

Jardine was a smooth talker, and Rimbow turned calculating eyes on him. A smooth actor, too, when it suited his purpose. Jardine's dark, clean-shaved face seldom revealed anything beyond the bland confidence of a thoroughly ambitious man used to having his own way.

With Rimbow's hard look on him, Jardine said, "I'm sorry about Mike, too, Rimbow, but business is business, Jim. Mike died owing me five hundred dollars."

"For what?" Rimbow demanded.

"Cash money. He wanted it real bad."

"Why?"

Jardine shrugged. "I suppose Mike had a case of cabin fever, staying by himself up there in the Hoot Owls so long. He wanted to blow off steam."

"Five hundred dollars worth?"

Jardine chuckled again. "The Irish are like that, Jim. They're a steamy breed."

It didn't make sense to Rimbow. He asked, "You got proof of the loan?"

Jardine nodded. "Mike put up half interest in your place as security." As Rimbow eyed him in disbelief, the other man went on: "I'll give you a thousand cash and take over your half of the place. No sense in you trying to run it alone."

Rimbow had disliked this man before, knowing that Jardine had long wanted his range in the Hoot Owls, but now he despised him. "You're not talking to a drunken man now, Jardine," he said flatly.

"But you stand to lose the place to the bank eventually," the rancher suggested.

"My business, and none of yours."

"Well, how much do you want for your half?"

"More than you've got," Rimbow said. "More than you'll ever have."

It was John Martin who chuckled now. He said, "That's well put, Jim." Glancing at Jardine he asked, "What's all the rush about? Jim hasn't been back long enough to get his bearings."

But Jardine was angry, and showed it in the way he peered at Rimbow, saying, "Unless that five hundred is paid within sixty days, I'm your partner, Rimbow."

Rimbow laughed at him. "Partner, hell!" he scoffed

and walked on along the street.

A drunken man, with a dented derby perched on the back of his head, stood propped against a rain barrel at the corner of Burro Alley. He clung to a valise with one hand and to a sample case, marked "Ajax Hardware," with the other.

"Where's the railroad depot at?" he asked foggily. "I've got to take a train east."

Rimbow motioned toward the alley, whereupon the hardware drummer mumbled, "Much obliged to you, friend."

He took an exploratory step from the rain barrel, skidded in a floundering turn and sat down with knee-buckling abruptness. A blond girl in a black silk kimono leaned from an upstairs window of the Fandango Dance-hall and laughed at the drunken man. Then, as Rimbow passed below her, she called, "What's your hurry, hand-some?"

"None of your damned business," Rimbow said, and turned into the Lady Gay Saloon.

Business was slow at this time of day. Three men stood at the long rosewood bar, all strangers to Rim-bow. Two others drank at a table midway between the gambling layouts, now deserted, and the dance floor at the rear. Another man, garbed in gambler's black broadcloth, sat at the piano, idly caressing the keys. Lew Tiffany, Rimbow observed, had brought some of the same fixtures that had been in his place at Abilene—and some of the same help. The florid-faced barkeep and the gaunt, sad-eyed man at the piano were both familiar.

As Rimbow's questing eyes sought Lew Tiffany and failed to find him, the man at the piano called, "No use waiting, Rimbow. Lew won't be back until after supper."

Rimbow thought, *So they've been expecting me...* and noted that Duke Hazelhurst hadn't changed at all. The card dealer still kept his pale fingers limber by tinkering at a piano when he wasn't playing poker.

Rimbow said, "Tell Lew I'll be back this evening."

"Sure," Hazelhurst said, his solemn face showing no interest at all. "I'll tell him." Then, as if it didn't really matter, he added: "Your friend O'Mara deserved what he got. He insulted the most beautiful woman in Arizona Territory. What he did could almost be called assault in a public place."

Rimbow rejected that with a slapping motion of his hand. "To hell with the woman," he muttered. "It's Tiffany I'm settling with. You tell him to start shooting when he sees me, so he won't be surprised when I do the same."

Some secret thought deepened the ruts on Hazelhurst's sallow cheeks. He said, "Perhaps you'll be the one who is surprised."

Rimbow wondered about that as he walked along Main Street. What was Duke hinting at? Certainly he wouldn't be alluding to the fact that Tiffany carried a hide-out gun in a shoulder holster. Anyone remotely acquainted with Lew Tiffany would guess that. Nor would Hazelhurst be apt to brag of his boss' gun skill. Tiffany might look lightning fast against a drunken man, but he was no world-beater. There were others as good, and some a damned sight faster. Yet Duke had suggested he might be surprised.

How could a tinhorn gambler surprise an ex-town marshal? It didn't make sense to Rimbow.

The drunken hardware drummer was on his feet again, and propped against the rain barrel. He faced east, his head canted to one side as if he were attempting to decide the exact location of an engine which was noisily chugging somewhere in the railroad yards.

"Where's the depot at?" he asked. "I've got to catch that train east. Very important!"

But Rimbow wasn't looking at him now. He was peering past the drunken man to where Lew Tiffany stood.

Then he was calling, "Turn around Tiffany—turn around!"

5

Gundown

THERE WAS a frown on Sheriff Pinky Weaver's round clean-shaved face as he rode westward along Main Street. Town living suited him just fine—its comforts had seemed miraculous to his wife after years of hard-scrabble existence on a poverty-plagued homestead. Pinky Weaver had been the most contented of men until the Chastain-Jardine feud broke into open warfare. That, and the subsequent boom in Reservation, had turned his law job into a still continuing nightmare.

When he came abreast of Martin's Mercantile the mayor called from the stoop, "Come here a minute, Pinky."

Weaver nodded acknowledgment, and because he could guess what the short, pudgy-faced merchant wanted, said impatiently, "I'm some in a hurry, John."

"As usual," Martin said dourly. "But you'd better take time to listen to this. The Citizens' Committee held a special meeting this morning. They agree with me that your enforcement of law and order isn't sufficient, and they want something done about it, quick."

"Well, I got no time to talk about that now. Doc

Carter's wife says there's been a shooting near Spade. Doc is on his way there."

"She say who got shot?"

"Old Hawk Halliday."

"Bad?"

"She didn't say."

As Pinky started to ride on, Martin asked, "What will I tell the committee?"

Weaver used a shirt sleeve to wipe his perspiring face. "I've told Lew Tiffany and them others to quiet down. I said there'd been too much noise and too much fighting, especially at night when decent folks want to sleep. But Tiffany says it's the miners and cowboys that make the noise and cause the trouble. He says it's them I should talk to, not the saloonkeepers."

"And you agreed with him?" Martin asked.

"Well, sort of. At least it's the miners and cowboys that make most of the rumpus."

Martin's face mirrored his disgust. "If I didn't know you're honest I'd think you were on Tiffany's payroll," he muttered. Then he asked, "Are you afraid of him, Pinky?"

Weaver shook his head. "But I ain't asking for a shootout with Lew Tiffany. What would that get me, except a bullet in the belly?"

"You're supposed to preserve law and order. That's what the county hired you to do."

"But not to be no boomtown city marshal," Weaver protested. "That ain't what I hired out for, and it ain't what I'm intending to be. I've got two deputies and they have to be jailers on twelve-hour shifts. I've got more county business than I can attend to without being at the beck and call of your Citizens' Committee." Riding on, Weaver called over his shoulder, "You can tell 'em I said so!"

Mayor Martin shrugged in the resigned way of a man finished with a futile chore. He had known what Pinky's attitude would be, and understood the uselessness of trying to change it. Pinky Weaver had a politician's knack of side-stepping trouble and following the lines of least resistance. He had shrgged off the Chastain-Jardine feud by saying a sheriff couldn't control range wars, which, Martin admitted, was true. Now Pinky shrugged off town law enforcement by saying he was no city marshal. And that was probably the truest thing he had ever said.

Pinky Weaver didn't have the grit, the guts or the gun skill to be a city marshal. Nor a shooting sheriff, for that matter. The voters had elected an honest homesteader to office, and that's exactly what they'd got.

It occurred to Martin that that was about all they had needed at the time. An honest man who'd keep an eye on petty rustlers and lock up an occasional drunk and serve legal papers. But the past few months had altered the need, and tremendously increased it.

Martin watched Lew Tiffany come down the Palace Hotel steps, a tall well-dressed man moving with the indolent assurance of an important personage. Which he was, Martin thought. Tiffany ran the most prosperous business in town. He hired the most help and paid the highest wages. Waiting for him now, Martin felt an odd mixture of resentment and envy.

"Good afternoon, Mayor," the gambler greeted, and gave his attention to lighting a cigar.

Martin nodded a wordless acknowledgment. He waited until Tiffany discarded the match before saying, "Our Citizens' Committee has decided to take action."

"Action?"

"Against you, and others whose places are causing trouble."

Tiffany exhaled tobacco smoke. He was a head taller than Martin so that now he looked down as he said, "Your attitude is all wrong, Mayor. My place causes no trouble. I start no fights, and my men start none. All we do is stop trouble when it comes."

"By killing the customer?"

The saloonkeeper deliberated a moment, then he said, "If it's forced upon us, yes. But not otherwise. In the case of Mike O'Mara I had no choice. Your sheriff admits that."

"Our sheriff is easily satisfied," Martin objected. "I think he's afraid of your gun."

Tiffany smiled. He asked pleasantly, "And you're not?"

While Martin considered the question and sought for an honest answer a voice called sharply, "Turn around, Tiffany—turn around!"

Martin glanced to where Jim Rimbow stood, his right hand poised an inch above the butt of his holstered gun.

Lew Tiffany asked urgently, "Is that Rimbow behind me?"

Martin nodded, and saw the gambler's face muscles

tighten. Yet he made no move for his gun.

"Step away from him, John," Rimbow called.

Until this instant it hadn't occurred to Mayor Martin that there might be a shootout. Now, as the significance of Rimbow's request came to him, Martin backed off with an alacrity that brought him into collision with a hitchrail. Ducking under it he continued out into the hoof-pocked dust.

That spasmodic retreat stirred a remote and cynical amusement in Jim Rimbow. It reminded him of the many times in Abilene when a city marshal's challenge had sent bystanders scurrying. Men forgot their dignity when fear clawed at them, regardless of the town they lived in, or with whom they sided. Men like Tiffany thrived on that cowardice.

There was something else here that was familiar—the sense of unreality and compression, the tension and tight focus clamping two men in hypnotic appraisal—as Lew Tiffany turned in the deliberate way of a man facing a task he disliked. Tiffany's broad bland face appeared pale in the fading sunlight and so did his hands, thumb-hooked in the pockets of a checkered vest.

He said, "Hello, Rimbow," in the tone of a man renewing a casual acquaintance.

"I hear you were too fast for Mike O'Mara," Rimbow said flatly.

Tiffany nodded and waited, motionless as a man could be.

Rimbow observed the telltale bulge of a gun under the unbuttoned coat. He said, "Let's see if you're too fast for me."

"Take it easy," the gambler suggested, his voice retaining a tone of measured civility. "There's no sense in us fighting each other, Rimbow. No sense at all."

"I say different," Rimbow announced. "I say we fight, here and now."

As he waited for the first blurred dart of Tiffany's hand, Rimbow recalled having heard that Tiffany also wore an armpit holster.

"It takes two to make a fight," Tiffany suggested, very calm in the way he spoke and very careful not to move.

Rimbow nodded. "There's two of us."

He heard a work train rumble into the railroad yards somewhere behind him, and wondered if the drunken hardware drummer had reached the depot, and was vaguely aware of a gathering crowd along both sides of Main Street.

"Come on," he urged. "You've got a gun. Start using it!"

The gambler's big hands came slowly away from his vest. He said quietly, "I'm not drawing against you."

Astonishment had its brief way with Rimbow. He stared at Tiffany in disbelief. Then a backwash of tension whipped through him. "You counterfeit!" he said rankly. "You yellow-bellied, stinking counterfeit!"

There was an instant when he thought Tiffany was going to draw. The gambler's cheeks went chalky and temper flared in his amber eyes. But the moment passed, and now Tiffany said again, "I'm not going to draw against you!"

Rimbow still couldn't believe it, couldn't comprehend

that so proud and arrogant a man would publicly profess cowardice, for that was what this amounted to. Lew Tiffany had built a career on boldness, and a brazen disregard of consequences. There was no meekness in the man, and no doubt of his ability with a gun. Yet now he was refusing to accept a rightful challenge; refusing to settle a legitimate score. It was past Rimbow's understanding.

Believing there must be a trick to it, Rimbow kept his right hand close to holster as he taunted, "So you'll only fight a drunken man?" Then, observing that perspiration moistened Tiffany's blond sideburns, he called, "Yellow as your hair, by God!"

Duke Hazelhurst and a Lady Gay bouncer named Billy Dial came across the street and moved in on either side of Tiffany. The gambler ignored them. He said to Rimbow, "You'll change your tune one of these days. You'll regret you ever called me yellow."

Rimbow laughed at him. "How about now?" he asked, and flicked a glance right and left to the men flanking Tiffany. "Don't three-to-one odds suit a tinhorn?"

But Tiffany refused the bait. Turning his back he walked away and his two men went with him, Billy Dial asking amazedly, "What's the deal, Lew—what's the deal?"

That was a question Jim Rimbow asked himself—Why had Tiffany turned yellow in the clutch? With two guns to back him, why had the gambler refused to fight?

It didn't make sense to Rimbow, but it seemed to make plenty of sense to Mayor Martin who came quickly over to him and exclaimed, "He remembered your Abilene reputation as a killer marshal, Jim!"

Other townsmen gathered around Rimbow now. Fritz Elmendorf shook his hand and said, smiling, "Never such talk have I seen a man take. A counterfeit you called him, and that he must be."

Fred Peppersall, proprietor of the feed store, clapped him on the shoulder and Pete Eggleston said happily, "As Keats wrote—he's the bane of every wicked spell, silencer of the dragon's yell."

Cash Bancroft came from his Apache Basin Bank and said something to Mayor Martin, who nodded agreement. Turning to Rimbow, Martin said urgently, "Reservation needs a city marshal, Jim, and you're the man for it."

A cynical smile quirked Rimbow's lips. He shook his head, saying, "I got enough of that in Abilene. More than plenty."

"We'll make it worth your while," Fred Peppersall urged.

Rimbow felt like laughing in his face. He was tempted to ask: *How do you know what it's worth to wake up in the night with a gun in your hand, not knowing how it got there . . . and cold sweat dribbling from your armpits. . . .* Did this feed store merchant have a method to measure the flinching and grinding of a town-tamer's guts when he walked down a dark street? Could he weigh the worry and apprehension that burdens a man who knows he is a target, day and night, week after week?

Fritz Elmendorf said coaxingly, "A big job big money pays, Jim."

Rimbow said, "I'll never need money bad enough to wear a badge again."

As he went on across the street the irony of Martin's offer brought a mirthless smile to his whisker-shagged cheeks. A few hours ago he had been a handcuffed prisoner of the law—now they were offering him a badge. Two days ago he had considered himself a prosperous man; now he could scarcely afford the new shirt and underwear he was going to buy at the Mercantile.

"City marshal, hell!" Rimbow muttered. There was just one chore he had to do here—visit Mike O'Mara's grave. And it didn't seem right to do it in a dirty shirt. A man bathed and shaved before he went to a funeral, Rimbow reasoned. He would show the same respect. He was turning into the Mercantile doorway when he collided with a gingham-clad woman who held a paper sack of groceries cradled in her arms.

Rimbow peered into a pair of startled gray eyes. He stood holding her with both hands, as if she were his dancing partner, while the fragrance of her hair came to him like an intimate perfume. Her lips, slightly parted and on the edge of smiling, were a ripe scarlet against the soft oval of her face.

"Would you mind releasing me, please?"

Her voice was low-pitched and casual, but her eyes, startlingly blue against long black lashes, held an aloofness. Rimbow steped back in the embarrassed fashion of a man caught dreaming in broad daylight.

You don't see a beautiful woman for months and then suddenly you have one in your arms. You forget there is creamy flesh so flawless or lips so inviting or eyes that give you a sense of immersion when you look into them. Baffled by all this, Rimbow bowed and said, "Excuse me, ma'am," and was stepping around her when she asked abruptly, "Are you Jim Rimbow?"

He nodded, halting beside her and observing a subtle change in her eyes, a darkening that gave them a moist, warm glow. They were, he thought, the eyes of a passionate and very lovely woman, and wondered who she was.

"I am sorry about Mike O'Mara," she said softly. "I am Marlene Lane."

The simple, sober statement was like a slap in the face to Jim Rimbow. He had pictured the woman for whose kiss Mike had died as being quite different. Despite Pete Eggleston's eloquent description he had tallied Marlene as the usual man-bait, a trollop trained to turn men's heads and excite them with her singing. But there was nothing wanton about this suddenly warm-eyed woman, no deviousness; her simple calico dress couldn't wholly conceal her ripe womanhood, but it bore no resemblance to the "low-and-behold" gowns styled for calculated revealment.

"I said I was sorry," she murmured. "Don't you believe me?"

"What difference does that make now?" Rimbow asked, and continued his speculative appraisal.

She was, he guessed, about twenty-five, and was made the way a woman should be, with a fullness of breast that accentuated the supple grace of a body that seemed tall, though came only to his chin. Her hair, drawn back in loose waves, was a rich russet color. It came to him that she was not pretty in the way he thought of prettiness, nor were her features beautiful exactly, now that he studied them. But there was a womanliness about her and a rare wholesomeness.

Marlene Lane met his deliberately appraising eyes with the calm assurance of a woman accustomed to being looked at, a woman aware of her attractions and capable of ignoring the inevitable attention they drew.

She said, "I tried to talk Mike into going back to the ranch. I tried to convince him that no good would come of his drinking and gambling. But he wouldn't listen to me."

"From what I've been told he listened to you every night," Rimbow said flatly. "Mike had a bad habit of mixing hard likker with soft women."

Rimbow expected to see resentment, or shame, to hear himself angrily denounced. For that would be the expected reaction of a professional wanton, implicated in a shooting which had cost a man his life. But there was no alteration in the composed serenity of her face, no sign of resentment in her calm gray eyes as she asked, "Do I look like what you call a soft woman?" And while he considered that: "Or do you mean a loose woman?"

That was exactly what he meant. And he understood she knew it. But looking at her now he couldn't call her loose, and so he said nothing.

Marlene's lips parted in a slow, bitter-sweet smile as she said, "Mike told me about you."

"So?"

"He said you were all man, and that you had no use

for women." Her eyes were unwavering on his as she added: "But he told me that you weren't nearly as tough as you talked and acted. I choose to believe he was right."

Then she turned and walked away, leaving Rimbow to watch the gentle rhythmic sway of her hips as she continued along the sunlit street. In this brief interval, while surprise and confusion had their way with him, Rimbow understood why Pete Eggleston had called her the image of a man's campfire dreams.

He thought it was no wonder Mike had fallen for her—she was enough to make any man have notions.

Because the admission stirred a rankling resentment in him, Rimbow muttered, "To hell with her," and went on into the Mercantile. But the memory of Marlene's warm eyes remained with him as he made his simple purchases, and the feminine scent of her was a lingering fragrance in his senses.

6

Call Me Killer

THE SUN had dipped behind the high ramparts of the Dragoons when Rimbow came out of the barbershop. A hot, soaking bath had relaxed him; a shave, haircut and clean clothing had been refreshing. Yet there was no buoyancy in him as he walked along the dusk-hazed street and turned south into Residential Avenue. Passing lighted homes Rimbow recalled the countless times he and Mike had eaten their evening meal together. The homestead would be a lonely place without a partner to share it, even if he could talk Cash Bancroft into extending the bank loan.

Entering the little cemetery with its white picket fence, Rimbow found Mike's grave by going to the first of three fresh mounds. He struck a match and held it to the wooden cross on which was carved: *Mike O'Mara, died Aug. 5, 1887.*

Rimbow peered at the inscription until the match burned his fingers. It still didn't seem real to him that Mike was dead. Even here, with Mike's name on a cross, it was difficult for him to accept the fact that his partner was gone. You ride with a man. You see the effortless way he flanks a calf or lifts a sack of feed. Strong as an ox, tough as whang leather, and damned alive. Then you are told he's dead. And buried. You look at a cross with his name on it. . . .

Rimbow took off his hat. A gentle evening breeze ruffled his hair. He felt a need to say something, to solemnize this moment in some fitting way. But all he said was, "Adios."

Afterward, walking toward Finucane's Livery, it occurred to Rimbow that he had not eaten since early morning. But there was no real appetite in him now and so he thought to have a late supper at home. He was into the livery stable doorway before he was aware of the men in Finucane's office: Mayor Martin, Cash Bancroft, Fritz Elmendorf and Fred Peppersall.

John Martin called, "Come in, Jim. We've been waiting for you."

And Monk Finucane, who sat on his cot alongside Peppersall, invited, "Have a seat."

Understanding that this was another meeting of the Citizens' Committee and guessing why it had been called, Rimbow shook his head.

"I'm saddling up."

"Where you going?" Martin asked.

"Home."

Cash Bancroft asked, "Are you planning to keep your place?"

Rimbow stared at him, wondering why Cash should ask such a question. "I'm planning to try," he said. "Any reason why I shouldn't?"

"Well, Riley Jardine was inquiring about the possibility of acquiring your interest—at some future date," Bancroft reported with the sly mildness of a man offering an opening wedge in a horse trade. "He holds what amounts to a five-hundred-dollar second mortgage against it."

While Rimbow absorbed the significance of this information, John Martin said, "We need a city marshal and you need the money, Jim."

And Bancroft said, "If you take the job I'll renew your note for another year so you'll have no worry on that account."

They were all watching him now. All waiting to see if the bait was tempting him now. Rimbow's face showed them nothing and now Fred Peppersall said, "You could take a day off now and then to look after your ranch and stock."

Rimbow felt a trap closing upon him. It was the money that counted, money he needed to save his place in the Hoot Owls.

"How about it?" Mayor Martin asked. "Does our offer interest you, Jim?"

Rimbow nodded. He said, "I'll work the job two months for five hundred dollars, payable in advance."

"In advance?" Martin echoed.

Rimbow said flatly, "In advance. You won't lose unless I get knocked down. In that case we both lose, which seems like a square deal all around."

He grew aware of footsteps behind him and Riley Jardine stepped into the office doorway. Jardine asked, "Five hundred in advance for what?"

Rimbow ignored him, and for a moment no one seemed

inclined to speak. Finally Martin said, "For wearing a city marshal's badge for two months."

Jardine went on into the office, so that Rimbow couldn't see the effect the explanation had had on him. "Nice wages," Jardine said. "Isn't that pretty steep for three weeks work?"

"Two months," Mayor Martin corrected impatiently.

"But the railroad construction camp will move on within three weeks," Jardine insisted with the assurance of a man wholly confident that his counsel was welcome. "After that what need will there be for a town-tamer?"

That seemed to impress Cash Bancroft, for now the banker asked, "How about one month, Jim, at two hundred fifty dollars in advance?"

Rimbow shook his head. "Five hundred, or nothing."

"Do not over details quibble," Elmendorf urged, shaking a dyestained finger at the banker.

Fred Peppersall said, "There's no telling how much of the riffraff will stay on here. They didn't all come with the railroad and they won't all leave with it."

"Are you referring to my crew?" Jardine asked arrogantly.

Peppersall shrugged. "If the boot fits, wear it. But I'll say this right now—it's not Tiffany's bunch that rides down this street at night shooting off guns. And it's not railroaders or miners. It's cowboys, by grab, and they should be taught some proper manners!"

Rimbow saw that register on Jardine's lamplit face as Circle J's owner stared hard at Peppersall and said angrily, "I'll not be slandered by you or any other man! I employ no riffraff at my ranch. I hired gunfighters, yes

—but only after Spade started using guns against my men."

"Riley, this is a Citizens' Committee meeting," Mayor Martin said impatiently. Turning to Bancroft he announced, "We voted to take action. Now I propose that we hire Jim at the price he asks. Do you second that motion."

"Yes," said Bancroft.

Martin glanced at the others, asked, "Are you in favor of it."

They were.

"Jim, if you'll come over to the store I'll give you a bank draft for five hundred dollars," Martin said.

"You've made a deal," Rimbow agreed. Turning to Jardine he asked, "Have you got Mike's mortgage note with you?"

"It's at the bank. There's no rush about paying it off. You've got sixty days."

"I'll pay it tonight."

Jardine shrugged. "Suit yourself," he said, and as if this were a matter too trivial for personal attention, added, "Settle it with the bank cashier tomorrow."

Afterward, in Martin's office at the Mercantile, Rimbow looked at the draft the mayor gave him. Five hundred dollars. Yet it didn't seem like money to him. Not compared with the small fortune he had possessed a couple of days ago.

He asked, "Any special instructions?"

"Yes, Jim. We want a midnight curfew. We want

every place in town closed promptly at twelve o'clock. That won't stop the fighting and carousing, but it will put a time limit on it. If the Lady Gay closes at midnight the others will follow Tiffany's lead." A self-mocking smile creased Martin's pudgy cheeks as he added, "This town has two mayors. One represents the respectable folks and the other represents the riffraff. Up until now the last has had all the best of it."

"Do I get a badge?"

Martin shook his head. "I've got none to give you. Never thought we'd need a city marshal. But I'll ask Bancroft to write up a legal commission for you tomorrow." As they walked back through the deserted store Martin predicted, "You should have no trouble with Tiffany. He's afraid of you, Jim. I never saw the beat of it."

"Me neither," Rimbow admitted. Then he asked, "How about Jardine's crew. I hear he has some wild ones working for him."

Martin nodded. "I'm surprised that Riley would hire such men. But he has hated Spade and all it stands for since the first year he moved into Apache Basin. Riley didn't have much then, except ambition. He tried to court Eve Chastain, but Sam run him off—called him a greasy-sack drifter. That's how it started."

"Before my time," Rimbow said. "Beats hell how much trouble women cause."

"Eve was just a teen-aged girl at the time. A flirty, prideful girl who liked to stir men up."

"Who are the wild ones Jardine hired?"

"Well, there's Red Nedrow, Zig Chisum and Kid

Antrim, all from Texas. And Joe Bodine, who got run out of New Mexico. They're in addition to Riley's regular crew."

"A nice bunch," Rimbow mused. "I met the three from Texas when I was in Abilene. And knew Chisum before, in the Brazos country."

"Riley calls it fighting fire with fire."

"Did Sam Chastain hire gunslicks?"

"No, but his men aren't Gentle Annies either. It was a Spade rider that set things off—by shooting a Circle J man who'd been warned to quit pushing Jardine cows onto Chastain's winter range. That's when Riley began importing a hardcase crew."

It was, Rimbow thought, an old story. Old as cows and grass and water. Old as ambition. He asked, "How often do Jardine's toughs come to town?"

"Saturday nights, mostly. But they drift in and out any time. Usually run in pairs."

Then, as if this were important, Martin said, "We want law and order enforced, Jim. But don't pick on Circle J riders just because you don't like Riley. I'm not saying to give them special privileges, but don't make your job any worse than it is. If you stir up trouble with them, along with the saloon crowd, it might be more than you can handle."

"My worry," Rimbow said. "Not yours."

Martin shook his head. "It'll be my worry if I pay five hundred for a dead city marshal. The taxpayers wouldn't like that at all."

The raw humor of it struck Rimbow. He loosed a gusty hoot of laughter and said amusedly, "So my death would be a financial loss to Reservation."

But presently, as he walked into the Palace Hotel dining room and sat down at a table, the humor of Martin's words faded and he thought morosely, *That's what I am in this town—a five-hundred-dollar gun with ears.*

7

Queen of the Night

CITY MARSHAL Rimbow made his first official call at the Alhambra where Pete Eggleston accepted the curfew ultimatum with philosophical good humor. "The way business is I could close at nine o'clock and lose no trade," he said. "Have a drink on the house."

Rimbow shook his head. "Got work to do. How many places in town, Pete?"

"Well, let's see. Lady Gay is the biggest and, according to Lew Tiffany, the best saloon between El Paso and Tucson. There's one more on Main Street, where the Gaviota Pass road takes off for the north. Blacky Pratt's Silver Dollar is in Burro Alley just beyond Simpson's blacksmith shop, and there's a canvas shack behind it where his girls hang out. Farther down is Tay Daecy's Shamrock. Tay has no girls but he's a slick Mick with a deck of cards. There's a couple small places across the alley, one on either side of the Fandango Dancehall which has a bar and is a trap if ever I've seen one. The others are along the railroad tracks on the new street where they built the railroad depot. Front Street they call it, although Back Street would be a better name.

There's two saloons, a shooting gallery and a pawn shop along with a hotel that's no better than a bawdy house."

Rimbow formed his mental picture of the district, recalling how it had been before the boom. There were no plank walks in Burro Alley, which was barely wide enough for two teams to pass. He glanced at his watch, observing that it was after nine o'clock, and now Doctor Carter came through the batwings.

The old medico put his black satchel on the bar, said, "The usual," and then looked at Rimbow. "Any idea who did the shooting, Jim?"

Rimbow shook his head. "How is Halliday?"

"Delirious. Bad concussion, and lost a lot of blood. But he'll recover."

"Soon?" Rimbow asked.

"Hard to say. He might regain consciousness in an hour, a day or a week. After that it's merely a matter of how long it takes his broken leg to knit."

Carter picked up his drink and said musingly, "Jeff kept mumbling about handcuffs. I couldn't make sense of it, but he seemed to think he was wearing handcuffs and wanted them taken off."

Rimbow thought instantly: *It was on his mind when the bullet hit him. . . .* and it might be the first thing he would ask about when he regained consciousness. Had his handcuffed prisoner been killed?

The warm night was breezeless, day's heat hanging on as Rimbow crossed Main Street's wide dust. Occasional shafts of lamplight cut sharply across the deep pools of darkness in Burro Alley where half a hundred vague shapes moved in the loitering way of men with no set

81

destination. Piano music came from the Fandango Dancehall and a woman's shrill voice called, "Come on, you gandydancers—show your stuff!"

Rimbow turned into the Silver Dollar, narrowly averting collision with a staggering drunk who warned, "Look where you're goin'!" A dozen men, railroad laborers by the look of them, lined the bar of this boxy canvas-walled room.

Blacky Pratt was polite enough, neither accepting nor rejecting the curfew rule. "I'll do what the others do," he said, and offered Rimbow a drink.

"Too early," Rimbow declined and went on along the alley.

A woman sat at an open window, so close that the perfume smell of her came to Rimbow as he passed. She said invitingly, "What's your rush, handsome?" and leaned out the window in a way that revealed the swell of her ample bosom above a low-cut bodice.

"Scat!" Rimbow muttered. Ignoring her profane remark he wondered if Mike O'Mara had squandered part of the borrowed five hundred dollars on her. Poetry Pete had said Mike had bought trinkets for Marlene. Probably for other females also.

His next stop was at the Shamrock, where Tay Daecy's reaction was similar to Pratt's, except that the old Irishman was more specific. "I'll close me doors when Lew Tiffany closes his. 'Tis bad enough him havin' that Marlene to attract trade away from a respectable establishmint like mine, without givin' him a preference in the hours as well."

"The Lady Gay will close promptly at midnight,"

Rimbow assured him, and this time, because Daecy's Celtic voice reminded him of Mike O'Mara, Rimbow accepted the offer of a free drink.

"Faith, and 'twould be a good thing for all concerned to close at midnight," Daecy insisted. "Thim miners from the Silver King should not be hellin' around half the night, nor thim railroad workers neither. 'Tis the girlie rigs that keeps them up so late. The poor misbegotten boobs keep thinkin' they'll find a prettier female in the next place, but it's their week's wages that the girlies take. 'Twas only this afternoon that Frank Murdock was complainin' about it to me, and him the big mogul of the construction gangs. Tay, he says, my gandydancers droop at their tamps like pimply-faced north-of-Ireland dudes and me spike men swing their mauls like spineless Englishmen. 'Tis a howlin' shame, he says, how thim buckos spend the night in town instead of in their beds gittin' of their needed rest."

Rimbow wasn't much interested, one way or another. Men—all men—seemed to have a basic need to abuse themselves at regular intervals in a quest for pleasure. It had been that way with the mountain men who tromped long miles across nameless ranges and forded nameless rivers to celebrate in annual rendezvous; it was the same with cavalry troopers and cowboys, miners, railroaders and all manner of men. Mike O'Mara, according to Jardine, had contracted a bad case of cabin fever and blown off steam to get over it.

"Thanks for the drink," Rimbow said and crossed the alley to call on Rose Ducharme, blond, broad-bosomed proprietress of the Fandango Dancehall.

Rose accepted his ultimatum with smiling gracious-
ness. She was, Rimbow thought, a natural-born madam,
the lusty, good-natured type of woman who looked
upon all men as playful animals needing feminine enter-
tainment. "Anything you say, Mister Marshal," she
agreed. "Stop around after midnight and meet my girls.
I've got some real nice ones."

"Nice?" Rimbow said, and continued on his rounds.

There was little traffic on Front Street at this hour.
Except for the chuffing commotion of a switch engine
in front of the railroad depot and a metallic clicking
of the telegrapher's instrument, this north side of town
was quiet. And mostly dark. Recalling other times when
he had walked alone in dark places, Rimbow felt a
familiar sense of depression, of being a hunter of fugitives and being hunted in turn. The pattern never
changed. There was always this false front of acceptance
at the start, of seeming acquiescence. No definite sign
of refusal. No outright resistance. But the pressures kept
building up, night after night, and the devious hints
became more frequent——a rope strung knee-high across
a dark alley to trip the law, a slop bucket dumped from
an upstairs window and, finally, unseen guns fired from
night-shrouded passageways.

Killer marshal, he thought. For the moment they re-
spected him and his reputation, *Mr. Killer Marshal.* . . .

Walking through Front Street's clotted shadows Rimbow had the transient feeling that he was back in
Abilene. There was the same taint of drifting smoke
here; the same aromatic stink of stables and beer kegs
and trash-littered back yards all merging into one

pervading odor. Town smells.

Walking without hurry but without hesitation, Rimbow made his rounds, arriving back on Main Street via Gaviota Road. In each place the curfew rule stirred the same reaction and the same bow to Lew Tiffany. What he did they would do. Both he and Lew were killers.

As Rimbow neared the Lady Gay's yellow bloom of lamplight he wondered what Tiffany's reaction would be. If the gambler's performance this afternoon was any indication he would probably accept the curfew rule in good grace. But despite Lew's seeming cowardice, Rimbow could not accept the fact that Tiffany was afraid of him. There was something else in the situation —something he couldn't identify.

When he came to the Lady Gay's stoop Rimbow stood for a moment surveying the street and absorbing its details. Three men stood together on the Palace Hotel veranda. They were facing this way, their features indistinct, but Rimbow thought: *Martin, Bancroft and Peppersall. . . .* Someone was playing the piano inside. Not Duke Hazelhurst, Rimbow decided, for it wasn't being done very well.

Two cowpunchers trotted their horses up to the hitch-rack and dismounted, one saying, "We're still in time to hear Marlene sing."

A man quartered across from the Kansas Cafe, unsteadily. Rimbow recognized him now as the drunken hardware drummer and wondered what had become of his sample case. The man leaned against a stoop post and mumbled, "Got to listen for the train."

Rimbow flipped a half-smoked cigarette into the street. And now, as he turned toward the saloon doorway, his right hand did a thing it had learned a long time ago—it nudged the gun upward a trifle in holster, so that it rode free in the leather.

Bracket lamps and three ornate chandeliers gave the long room a brightness that was in sharp contrast to the dark street—in the moment while Rimbow's eyes focused in accommodation he knew a momentary wonder at the crowd this place had attracted. Two perspiring bartenders dispensed drinks to a solid rank of customers. Three of the five poker tables were occupied, a faro bank and roulette wheel were in operation and half a dozen couples danced to the combined music of a piano, accordion and guitar. Even though it wasn't a capacity crowd, Rimbow was astonished that there should be this much trade on a week night.

A percentage girl came up to him, smiling and asking, "Dance, Mr. Marshal?"

Rimbow shook his head, and now observing Lew Tiffany at the bar's front elbow, walked over to him.

The big gambler showed him a speculative gravity. "So you're a town marshal again," he mused, as if unable to comprehend a fact that baffled him.

Rimbow nodded. "Mayor Martin has placed a twelve o'clock curfew on the town."

"So I've heard," Tiffany said. His gambler's eyes revealed nothing, but his voice held a note of amusement when he asked, "Why did you come here last, instead of first?"

"Because I wanted the other places to understand

that I'm running the town, not you," Rimbow said bluntly.

Billy Dial got down from his high stool behind the faro bank and started across the room but Tiffany motioned him back. Duke Hazelhurst, handling the stick at the roulette wheel, kept glancing Lew Tiffany's way, and Rimbow thought, *Something's in the wind.*

"You're to close at twelve o'clock sharp," he told the saloonkeeper.

Tiffany said, "I'll be glad to cooperate, if you'll do the same."

"What do you mean by that?"

"I'll close every night at twelve, except Saturday. That night we throw away the key."

So that was it. Tiffany knew that one Saturday night was worth half a dozen other nights. And he was tempting a town marshal—offering him an easy way to enforce an unpopular curfew. Instead of meeting opposition head on, Tiffany was bargaining with the skill of an accomplished horsetrader.

"No," Rimbow said. "You close every night at twelve."

Tiffany didn't like that and showed it in the tone of his voice as he said, "I let you get away with a raw deal this afternoon. The rawest deal I've ever seen."

"Why?" Rimbow asked, sincerely curious to know the reason.

Tiffany shrugged. A down-curving smile quirked his broad lips and he said, "I had a good reason—you can be sure of that. But don't push a man too far."

"A man?" Rimbow asked, and took secret satisfaction in the ruddy flush that stained Tiffany's cheeks. "I'm telling you to close this trap tonight and every night at twelve o'clock."

For a long moment Tiffany considered that in the thoughtful way of a man reaching a difficult decision. Finally he asked, "And if I don't close down at twelve?"

Jim Rimbow kept a tight rein on himself. He tried to keep his personal feelings out of it, to ignore the fact that this bland-faced, prosperous gambler had shot down Mike O'Mara. But the need for vengeance was still strong in him and so he said, "I'll shoot out your goddam lights."

At this moment, as Tiffany absorbed that warning, the fat, derby-wearing man at the piano announced: "Ladies and gentlemen!"

A burly railroader at the bar asked loudly, "Did you say ladies?"

The subsequent burst of laughter was renewed when a percentage girl shrilled, "And where's the gentlemen at?"

The fat piano player ignored his hecklers. "For the fifteenth consecutive night it is my very great privilege and profound pleasure to present the most melodious, the most beautiful, and the most talented lady east or west of the Pecos—Marlene!"

Rimbow observed that Tiffany joined in the spontaneous applause. As Marlene came through a small side door near the piano, Rimbow sensed the instant alteration her presence made in this place. A moment ago there had been ribald humor and typical saloon hilarity, yet in the fleeting interval while Marlene took her place beside the piano the attitude of these applauding men changed to something else entirely.

TEXAS GUNS

No silver sequins glittered on the black gown Marlene wore. No jeweled combs decorated the rich, russet glory of her hair, no bracelets circled her round bare arms, no necklace broke the pure line of a throat that rose swanlike from unadorned shoulders. There wasn't a frill or a furbelow to accentuate cut or curve of the gown; no trinket to enhance the feminine lure of the woman who wore it. Almost, Rimbow thought sourly, it was as if she wore nothing at all, so strongly did the simplicity of her dress set off her physical charms. Well, it was a new twist.

Marlene smiled and raised a hand in comradely salute and waited for the applause to die down. When it did, her husky, low-toned voice came across the smoke-draped saloon. "Thank you very much."

Rimbow was aware of her gaze briefly touching him, or Tiffany—he could not be sure which of them she smiled to. But he heard Tiffany say, "What a woman!"

Marlene stood for a moment, showing the crowd a bitter-sweet smile of appreciation that gently curved her moist lips. Rimbow thought, *This is how Mike saw her* . . . and understood exactly how it was with his dead partner. A romantic man could go pure loco over a woman like that, and a romantic Irishman, who liked all women simply because they were women. . . .

Marlene introduced her first song by saying, "This is in memory of a man who liked to sing, and to hear others sing."

And then she was singing a song that affected Jim Rimbow hugely—Mike O'Mara's favorite tune: *Garry Owen.*

Singing it with an effortless ease in a lilting, low-pitched voice melodious as mission bells . . .

> *Let Bacchus' sons be not dismayed,*
> *But join with me, each jovial blade;*
> *Come booze and sing, and lend your aid*
> *To help me with the chorus.*

It was an astonishing thing. Jim Rimbow, who had threatened to slap a saloon singer named Marlene, barely kept from joining the voices around him as they sang:

> *The sky was blue,*
> *The grass was green,*
> *And a finer horse was never seen.*
> *Oh, his name was G-a-r-r-y O-w-e-n!*

Turning abruptly away from the bar, Rimbow walked out of the Lady Gay and tried to shut his ears to Marlene's voice as she sang another stanza:

> *Instead of Spa we'll drink down ale,*
> *And pay the reckoning on the nail;*
> *No man for debt shall go to jail*
> *From Gar-r-ry—Owe-en in glo-ree-ee!*

Out on the stoop Rimbow came face to face with the Ajax Hardware drummer who stood as a man in a trance. "What a voice," he said, and then added: "What a woman!"

Walking toward the Palace Hotel, Rimbow remembered how Poetry Pete Eggleston had described Marlene's singing. It hadn't made sense to him then, but it did now, and because he saw this appreciation as a weakness, Rimbow cursed himself for a woman-wanting fool.

8

Law of the Night

MAYOR MARTIN, Cash Bancroft and Fred Peppersall were still waiting on the Palace veranda. As Rimbow came up the steps Martin asked, "What did Lew Tiffany say?"

"He offered to close at twelve if I'd let him throw away the key on Saturday night," Rimbow said.

The three men considered that in silence for a moment, then Bancroft said, "Well, that's much better than it's been," and seemed satisfied.

"But that's the night they raise most of the hell," Peppersall protested. "How can decent folk sleep with a bunch of damned drunks prowling the streets until all hours?"

Martin said, "Reverend Pendergast's church group won't like that at all. They maintain that the Sabbath starts at one minute past twelve on Sunday morning and that it should be properly observed."

Amused at the way this was going, Rimbow inquired, "Is your wife a member of that group, John?"

The mayor nodded.

"So is mine," Bancroft said thoughtfully.

"And mine," added Peppersall.

Rimbow took out his Durham sack and rolled a cigarette, content to let them stew. He supposed that these men's wives were the motivating force behind the twelve-o'clock curfew, for that was the usual pattern. Men, he had observed, were generally not much interested in civic virtue or desecration of the Sabbath.

As if reluctant to say this, Mayor Martin asked, "Did you agree to Tiffany's proposition?"

Rimbow shook his head. "I told him to close every night at twelve, or else."

"Good!" Martin exclaimed.

"Or else what?" Bancroft inquired.

"Or I'd shoot out his lights."

"That's fine," Martin said, genuinely pleased. "I'm glad you were strict with him, Jim. Pinky Weaver tried being lenient and accomplished nothing."

"Will Tiffany close tonight?" asked Bancroft.

Rimbow nodded. "One way or the other."

In the moment while they considered this a woman at the corner of Burro Alley cried, "Marshal Rimbow!"

"Trouble," Rimbow muttered.

As he went down the steps the shrill voice called urgently, "Help—send the marshal!"

There wasn't much doubt in Rimbow's mind as to what he would find in Burro Alley. Some drunk, he supposed, had gone berserk and some bawd was screaming for help. But now, as he neared the opposite sidewalk, an abrupt wonderment came to him—why hadn't the woman called on a bouncer, or friends in the alley for help? Why had she come out to Main Street and summoned a marshal who'd scarcely been in office an hour?

It didn't add up, unless there was an additional motive—a hidden gun waiting for a target. Rimbow veered sharply, continuing along Main Street's dust where his boots made no sound as he walked past the alleyhead. There was no break in the quilt of darkness here, but lamplight bloomed from a dozen doorways in Burro Alley and nothing in the alley stirred.

Sure now that the alley was a baited trap, Rimbow went on toward Finucane's Livery. He was turning into the wagonyard when Monk came up and asked sleepily, "Did ye hear a woman scream for help?"

"Yes, but I think she was funning."

"Didn't sound comical to me," Finucane protested. "She woke me up. I'm going to take a look."

"Stay out of Burro Alley," Rimbow commanded. "Don't go near it."

He went on into the wagonyard, felt his way to the rear fence and climbed over it. A narrow passageway here, he remembered, opened onto Burro Alley between Pratt's Silver Dollar Saloon and the blacksmith shop. Peering ahead Rimbow observed a remote glow of lamplight through canvas. That, he supposed, was the girlie shack Eggleston had mentioned. Crossing the trash-littered passageway cautiously, he cat-footed into the deeper darkness behind the blacksmith shop and held to it until he had gone beyond the shack's faint illumination. Turning again he felt his way along the rear of the shop, came to its corner and stopped. Ahead of him was the lesser darkness of Burro Alley.

Rimbow scouted the opening and saw nothing to bolster his suspicion. But the belief that this was a logical location for ambush remained strong in him and it was nourished by the continued, unaccustomed stillness of the alley. No sounds came from the lighted doorways or even from the girlie shack.

Sharply focusing his eyes on the saloon's blank wall, Rimbow gave the front corner a continuing scrutiny. For a long moment he detected no sign of any kind. He thought, *Maybe I'm loco* . . . and wondered if habitual wariness had tricked him into a fool's errand. Then he glimpsed something that banished the thought completely: a slight alteration in the pattern of deep shadow along the saloon wall—a barely discernible movement that allowed him to identify a shape that made a denser shadow against the opaque darkness.

There was a man there. A man who had moved an elbow, or perhaps shifted his weight from one foot to another. But he was there, and Rimbow needed no further sign to know why he was there. They weren't waiting to build up pressure against him. Somebody had decided to silence a five-hundred-dollar gun quickly, before it cut into the profits.

Rimbow edged slowly ahead, a careful step at a time. The waiting ambusher, he guessed, had about given up hope of a target, for he moved again, and now there was the flare of a match as he lighted a cigarette.

Acting instantly, Rimbow ran forward. The man turned, his cigarette tip glowing briefly in the split second before it dropped from his lips. Rimbow used it for a target and swung his gun barrel at the man's head.

There was a wheezing grunt as the man went down. Rimbow didn't know the dry-gulcher had drawn his gun until it exploded, the unaimed bullet ripping along the saloon wall. Rimbow dropped, using his weight on the man's sprawled body and seeking the gun. There was no resistance now.

The three members of the Citizen's Committee on the hotel veranda heard the shot, barely audible above music from the Lady Gay. For a moment they stood listening, thinking there might be another. Then Mayor Martin said, "Jim Rimbow has made his first arrest."

"Or his last try to make one," Fred Peppersall suggested ominously.

They waited in silence for another interval. Finally Cash Bancroft said, "Maybe we'd better go see what happened. He may need help."

"Not the kind we can give him, without a gun," Peppersall scoffed. "What good would we be?"

Then Rimbow came into the lamplight with a limp body draped over his left shoulder in the way a man totes a loosely-filled sack of grain.

"What happened?" Mayor Martin demanded.

"Pistol-whipped him," reported Rimbow.

"Why?" Bancroft asked.

"Resisting arrest."

"What's he charged with?"

Rimbow thought about that for a moment, understanding he had no legal evidence that his prisoner had intended to shoot him.

96

"Loitering," he said.

"But we've got no rule against loitering in this town," Martin protested.

"I have," Rimbow announced. "It reads that there's going to be no loitering in dark alleys with pistols, shotguns or other weapons."

Martin reached out and tilted the man's blood-smeared face to the lamplight. "Sid Fisher, who runs the poker game at the Silver Dollar." Then he asked, "What happened to the woman who called for you?"

"Why, she was just funning," Rimbow said and, walking on toward the courthouse, suggested, "You might send Doctor Carter over to find out how hard I hit Fisher."

"I'll go get him," Martin said and hurried off toward Residential Avenue.

Peppersall and Bancroft followed Rimbow, the banker saying, "His first arrest." And then, as if this made it more impressive, he added, "Without so much as a legal commission in his pocket."

"Jim's gun is his commission," Peppersall said. "It's one those toughs can read and understand." But while his voice held relief, it held apprehension also.

At eleven o'clock Rimbow returned alone to the Palace Hotel veranda, walking in the deliberate way of a man keening the night's shadows for what they might hold. The jailer, predicting that Fisher was fatally hurt, had gotten Bancroft and Peppersall excited. It was a curious thing how concerned law-abiding citizens became when an arrested rascal showed the least sign of dying. Rimbow took a chair, propped his boots on the veranda railing and lit his cigar. That deal in the dark passageway had been a trifle closer than he liked—if Fisher had been a bit faster, or less careless, it might now be he the Citizens' Committee was concerned about.

I should've shot him instead of pistol-whipping him, Rimbow thought. It would have ended the matter. This wasn't the first time he had taken his chances, rather than risk killing a man, and it probably wouldn't be the last; yet he was called a killer marshal. Remembering Hawk Halliday's accusation that he shot first and talked afterward, Rimbow swore softly. You were damned if you did, and damned if you didn't.

Mayor Martin and Doctor Carter came along the plank walk now, Martin asking fretfully, "Did Fisher regain consciousness?"

Rimbow shook his head.

"You think he's going to die?" asked Martin.

Rimbow shook his head again and watched them hurry off toward the jail. Martin, he thought, was like most good-citizen mayors—they wanted the law enforced, but disliked the violence of enforcement. They hired accomplished peace officers but shrank from the gun skill that made them effective. In all the time he had worn the star in Abilene no respectable citizen had invited him into his home for supper or introduced him to his wife. It would be the same here.

Presently he saw Marlene Lane come from the Lady Gay's side door, followed by Lew Tiffany. A cape was draped over her shoulders; that, and the way her sorrel hair shone in the lamplight, and the way she walked, gave her a regal appearance as Tiffany escorted her across the street. But Rimbow thought bleakly, *The pair of them caused Mike to die.*

When they passed the veranda Marlene looked at Rimbow, nodded and said pleasantly, "Good evening, Marshall."

Rimbow nodded acknowledgment, not speaking or smiling as they went on into the darkness.

A horse, trotting into town from the west, attracted his attention. Was it a Spade rider come to announce the fact that Jim Rimbow was wanted for murder? Had Hawk Halliday regained consciousness and sent word of an escaped prisoner? How, he wondered, would Mayor Martin and his Citizens' Committee react to the situation? Or, more importantly, how would Reverend Pendergast and his church women react to it?

The rider turned in at Finucane's Livery and dismounted in the lantern-lit doorway. As he unsaddled, Rimbow caught the reflection of the silver star on his vest and thought, Sheriff Weaver. He understood at once where Pinky had been.

Lew Tiffany, returning along the opposite side of the street, spoke to Weaver and came on to the Lady Gay. Rimbow took out his watch, saw that it was now twenty minutes to twelve, and wondered what Tiffany would do. If the Lady Gay was to close at midnight the bar should stop serving drinks now, and the gambling layouts should cash in their chips.

Pinky Weaver came on, seemingly headed toward the Lady Gay, but changed his mind and crossed the street, asking, "Is that you, Rimbow?"

"Yes."

"Monk Finucane says you've been made city marshal."

Rimbow nodded.

"He says you've told Tiffany to close down at midnight."

Rimbow nodded again.

"You reckon he'll do it?"

"One way or another," Rimbow said, and as two cowboys came out of the Lady Gay, he thought maybe it would be the easy way. When half a dozen more customers came out of the place, Rimbow knew it would be.

He said to Pinky, "Lew is a reasonable man. He likes to cooperate."

"He does?" Weaver asked, obviously baffled.

"In fact," Rimbow said soberly, "he's one of the most cooperative saloonkeepers I've ever met."

Sheriff Weaver gawked at the crowd spilling out of the Lady Gay. Very frank about this, and hugely puzzled, he said, "I never thought Lew Tiffany would do it. Not without a big fight."

As the Lady Gay's customers drifted off in various directions, Rimbow asked, "You been out to Spade?"

Weaver nodded.

"How's Halliday?"

"He was still unconscious when I left, soon after supper. I rode over to Circle J's line camp on Big Meadow. Chastain thinks those two men are the ones who ambushed Halliday. He wanted them questioned."

"Find out anything?"

Pinky shook his head. "They're a tough pair for sure. Cussed me out for coming to their camp after dark. Said next time they'd shoot and ask questions later."

"What's their names?"

"Red Nedrow and Joe Bodine."

Rimbow asked, "What does Bodine look like?"

"Well, he's medium built and some beefy in the face. A hard hombre if ever I saw one."

Rimbow recognized the dry-gulcher who had freed him from his dead pony.

"You ever met Bodine?" Weaver asked.

"One time, I think," Rimbow admitted, and remembering his promise to a dry-gulcher who had shot Halliday, wondered what would happen when Bodine learned he was city marshal.

The three big chandeliers in the Lady Gay were turned out, one at a time.

Pinky said, "Who'd of thunk it." As the bracket lamps went out, one after the other, he smiled and announced, "I'm glad they made you marshal, Jim. It's a load off me for sure."

"Shouldn't wonder," Rimbow mused. Then he asked, "Have you got an extra deputy badge I could borrow. Mayor Martin has no marshal badge for me to wear, and I'd feel better with one."

"Sure," Pinky agreed. "I'll go get it for you right now."

The hardware drummer came up the steps, narrowly missing collision with Weaver who hurried off toward the courthouse. The drunken man said forlornly, "Everything closed up—even the railroad depot."

He staggered into the lobby and Rimbow heard him

101

complain to the night clerk about the lack of train service. The clerk said impatiently, "I told you there was no regular passenger service yet. Why don't you take the stage?"

"Too slow, and too rough," the drummer said. "I've got a delicate stomach. Awful delicate."

Presently, as Sheriff Weaver came back to the veranda and handed Rimbow a silver star, he said, "Sid Fisher is still unconscious. Doc Carter says he may have a fractured skull."

"I should've used a bullet on him," Rimbow muttered. He pinned the badge on his shirt pocket and said, "Much obliged, Pinky."

Weaver said, "That's all right. Maybe you'll do me a favor some time."

"Such as what?" Rimbow asked.

"Well, take it a little easy with Riley Jardine's crew. Those boys get a little noisy, but they don't mean nothing by it."

Rimbow unpinned the star. He said, "No, thanks," and handed it back.

Weaver didn't take the badge. He asked, "You intending to arrest Circle J riders?"

"If they disturb the peace."

Weaver shrugged. "Well, all right then. Jardine helped me get elected and I'm beholden to him for it. But you ain't, Jim. Keep the badge."

He turned and walked toward Residential Avenue.

Rimbow looked at his watch. Twelve o'clock. He had rented a front room with what appeared to be a comfortable bed and was tired enough to use it. But there was one more round to be made.

A few drunks loitered in Burro Alley, bewildered by the closing of their favorite haunts. A few lights were on in the closed establishments where barkeepers and card sharps cashed in the day's take. Totting up the loot, Rimbow thought, and they'd be resenting the fact that it was less than usual because of the early closing. A curfew-enforcing city marshal would become increasingly unpopular in this town. Especially on Saturday night. That would be the real test of Lew Tiffany's cooperation, Rimbow understood. And it was only three nights away.

Front Street was dark, save for a lamp in the Elite Hotel lobby. When Rimbow turned into Gaviota Road he smelled fresh dust and wondered about it until he recalled the two cowboys. There would be plenty of riders in town Saturday night, he supposed, some of Jardine's Texas toughs among them.

The saloon on the corner was dark, which made the curfew complete.

One day of it done, Rimbow thought and walked on to the hotel.

9

AT 11 A.M. Marshal Jim Rimbow ate his late breakfast in the hotel dining room. Blacky Pratt, sharing a table with two other men, came over to Rimbow and asked, "What's the idea of pistol-whipping a man on a charge of loitering."

Ignoring the question, Rimbow asked, "Which one of your girls did the yelling act?"

"What you talking about?"

"About a rigged deal that backfired," Rimbow said crossly and looked him in the eye. "A stinking ambush if ever I saw one."

"Can you prove it?" Pratt inquired.

"Don't need to," said Rimbow and sampled his fried eggs.

Pratt stood there for a moment longer, as if wanting to say more and not sure how he should say it. Finally he muttered, "You might've killed him."

"Should've," Rimbow said, "and next time I will."

Pratt went back to his table. He and his companions eyed Rimbow with a continuing animosity so plain that the pressure of it was a tangible thing in this room.

104

The story of Sid Fisher's pistol-whipping had been spread all over town, Rimbow supposed, made more dramatic by the fact that he'd been unconscious for several hours. The saloon crowd would play it up as proof that Reservation's new city marshal was a trouble-maker—a zealot who went out of his way to stir things up. And the church crowd, wanting peace and quiet at any cost, would be wondering if such tactics were necessary.

Duke Hazelhurst came into the dining room, nodded a wordless greeting to Rimbow, spoke briefly to Pratt and took a table nearby. He was an odd one, Hazelhurst. Some past misfortune or quirk of character had turned him into a gambler, yet he retained the traits of a fastidious gentleman in the way he wore his well-tailored clothes and in the language he used. He seemed wholly out of place with such men as Blacky Pratt or Lew Tiffany, or Billy Dial who now came in and joined Hazelhurst. The contrast between these two employees of the Lady Gay was startling, for Billy Dial was a typical saloon bouncer with all the markings of casual brutality that trade put on its practitioners.

Dial had only a scowl for the new city marshal, but he greeted the Pratt trio with frank friendliness, inquiring, "Have you heard how Sid is this morning?"

"Conscious," Blacky Pratt reported. "But the medico says Sid had a narrow squeak."

"Hell of a thing," Dial muttered.

Rimbow thought angrily: *But it would've been a real smart thing if Sid had succeeded. . . .* The toughs and pimps and tinhorns knew how to hand out brutality but they couldn't take it without whimpering. Finished with his breakfast, he sauntered out to the lobby and bought a cigar. This, he realized, was to be his routine for sixty days—breakfast at eleven, an hour's leisure before going on active duty at noon; then twelve hours of wearing the star—of fending off the animosities and pressures of a hostile town that would dislike him a little more each day. And that dislike, he understood, eventually would be shared by the men who had hired him. For that was the price a town-tamer paid if he lived.

A hint of what was to come was waiting for him at the bank where he traded Martin's draft for the mortgage note Mike had signed. Cash Bancroft said, "Fisher claims he merely went out to the alley for a little fresh air—that he was just standing there when you hit him."

"Did he mention having a gun, which he fired?" Rimbow asked.

The banker shook his head. "But I think you might've made an inquiry before hitting him so hard."

"Your privilege to think as you please," Rimbow said flatly and walked out of the bank.

Later, while he sat on the hotel veranda, the Tombstone stage rumbled into town, and Rimbow gave its three men passengers a close scrutiny. One of them seemed to fit the brief appraisal Jube Tanner had given him—that Worden had "acted like a man who'd take your place." This stranger had a tough, back-trail look to him. Despite the fact that he wore a new Stetson and what appeared to be a recently acquired blue serge suit, he looked as if there might be a stink of campfire smoke in his bushy black hair.

He toted a small valise and now, as he came up the veranda steps, a rising sense of anticipation quickened Rimbow's pulse. If this should be Worden there'd be a weighty cargo of gold eagles in that valise—whatever Worden hadn't yet spent of fifteen hundred dollars or more!

The need to get his hands on the valise—to test its weight and, if it proved heavy, to open it—brought Rimbow out of his chair at once. Intending to follow the man into the hotel lobby, he was surprised when the stranger turned to him and asked, "Where can I find Hawk Halliday?"

The unexpectedness of it set Rimbow back on his heels.

"Who wants to see him?"

"Johnny Behman," the stranger said, and drawing asdie his coat, revealed a deputy sheriff's star. "From Tombstone."

Rimbow guessed why he was here. The stage driver must have reported Jube Tanner's murder and told about Hawk's being a passenger that far.

"Halliday is at Spade," said Rimbow. "He got ambushed and was still unconscious when Pinky Weaver left there last night."

The news plainly surprised Behman. "Why would anyone ambush Halliday?" he demanded as if such a thing were an affront to a Tombstone deputy's intelligence.

Rimbow shrugged. "Chastain seems to think it was

some of Riley Jardine's Texas gunslingers."

Behman considered that in silence for a moment. Then he said, "The murder of Jube Tanner wouldn't have any connection with range trouble up here."

"You say Tanner was killed?" Rimbow asked as if surprised.

"Robbed and murdered in cold blood. Hawk Halliday got off a westbound stage and discovered the corpse. Then he took out after the bandits."

"Afoot?"

"Borrowed one of Tanner's horses. I wanted to ask him what he found between Tanner's and here."

"A bullet," Rimbow said. "Couple of them, according to Doc Carter, who patched him up."

"Is Pinky Weaver in town?"

"Suppose so. Probably at his office."

"Go tell Pinky I want to see him, *muy pronto*," Behman ordered.

Rimbow shook his head. "Don't let this deputy sheriff's badge fool you," he suggested. "I'm city marshal here, not an errand boy."

Behman looked at him with a fresh interest. As if thinking aloud, he said slowly, "So you believe deputy sheriffs are just errand boys."

"No," Rimbow said, "but you seem to."

For a long moment they eyed each other in the way of strange dogs with raised hackles, then Behman shrugged and said, smiling, "No offense intended."

"None taken," Rimbow agreed. Behman went on into the hotel lobby.

Rimbow returned to his chair. He propped his feet

on the railing, but there was no ease in him, no relaxation. Wearing a star in this town was like being a cocked gun, he thought morosely. Not bad enough to have the riffraff putting on the pressure; you had to take it from visiting badge-toters. By God, it was enough to make a man bog his head. Behman, he supposed, would go to Spade. And if Halliday had regained consciousness, the Tombstone deputy's presence would bring things to a showdown. No doubt of it, nor of how the deal would shape up in case Halliday was able to tell what he knew—or thought he knew. When Behman heard the story he'd hightail to town and bring pressure to bear on Pinky Weaver to arrest a wanted murderer. Visualizing how that would be, and the jubilation it would cause among the saloon bunch, Rimbow swore softly. He'd have the choice, of course, of leaving town and going on the dodge.

At this moment he despised himself for having played a part in saving Hawk Halliday. The old lawman was the only one who knew he had been at Tanner's place the day Jube died, Rimbow thought. But he had to qualify that, for Worden had been there also.

Deputy Sheriff Behman came out of the lobby and stood for a moment on the veranda, seemingly interested in the considerable traffic on Main Street.

"Town's boomed since the last time I was over here," he reflected.

"A boomtown for sure," Rimbow agreed.

He watched Behman walk to the courthouse, and when he reappeared ten minutes later, knew exactly what the next move would be. As if watching the slow-motion building of a gallows for himself, Rimbow observed Behman's purposeful passage along the opposite sidewalk to Finucane's Livery, and his departure in a buckboard drawn by a team of matched bays. The Tombstone manhunter wanted to travel fast, but in comfort.

Rimbow looked at his watch. Eleven-forty-five. Judging the time it would take Behman to reach Spade, he thought the deputy wouldn't return much before five o'clock.

Afterward, making his first round of the town, Rimbow visited the new railroad depot and talked briefly with the telegraph operator who gave him the latest gossip. "Work is being held up because of a shortage of crossties and bridge timbers," the brasspounder reported. "Unless they get a new supply here quick the work will have to shut down—which means this construction camp may be stalled right here for several weeks."

That was more bad news for Rimbow. He had been inclined to agree with Riley Jardine's opinion that when the construction camp moved, most of the saloon bunch would go with it. "I hope they get their crossties in a hurry," he said, but presently, walking along Front Street, it occurred to him that it might not make any difference one way or the other. Five hours from now he might be lighting a shuck for the Border.

Dust churned up by passing wagons merged with smoke from a switch engine. The billowing haze had turned tawny by noon's brassy sunlight. When Rimbow passed the Railroad Saloon he heard one of the loafers in the doorway remark, "That's the lawdog who pistol-whipped Fisher," and another man said something that ended with "—meaner'n a sack of snakes."

Out on the flats a ranch wagon stirred up a trailing smear of dust and beyond that were the sunlit hills leading up to Gaviota Pass. He couldn't see the Hoot Owls, which lay west of the pass and fifteen miles north of it. But he could visualize their timbered slopes and high meadows, their remote, unbroken stillness. There was no dut up there, no smoke or nose or pressure, just quiet....

As Rimbow came abreast of the Elite Hotel veranda a fat man with a toothpick between his lips leaned over the railing and asked, "Does this burg remind you of Abilene?"

Rimbow halted, peering at the derby-wearing dude for a full moment before saying, "Real-estate Rand. What are you doing here?"

"Selling lots to them that have the sense to buy," Rand said, smiling. "This is going to be a big city, Jim—a regular metropolis."

Rimbow grinned, recalling how optimistic this man had been about Abilene real estate. A sort of jack-of-all-professions, Rand had been a dentist and a lawyer before becoming a high-pressure salesman.

"You opening up a land office here?" Rimbow inquired.

"Tomorrow, smackdab on Main Street in that new building next to the bank."

"Well, good luck."

"You too," Rand offered. "From what I hear you'll be

111

needing it before long, friend."

"So?"

Rand lowered his voice and said confidentially, "I've heard it said you'll not be around to enforce a twelve o'clock curfew Saturday night." He winked. "I heard it said you'd better live fast—for you won't live long."

"Just wishful thinking," Rimbow scoffed and walked on. But the warning reminded him that his big test was yet to come. This was Thursday. Two more nights, unless Behman's return to town interfered, then Saturday.

His leisurely round included a visit with Poetry Pete Eggleston and another with Tay Daecy. Judging by what these two proprietors told him, the town's opinion was as he had guessed it would be—that Fisher's arrest was merely a new marshal's method of showing that he was on the job. From past experience Rimbow could quote, almost word for word, what was being said—some would be apprehensive, others outright condemning.

And the Citizen's Committee, impressed by the critical opinion, would be wondering if they had hired a peace officer or a trouble-maker. Sauntering back to the Palace veranda, Rimbow thought, *To hell with what they say. . . .*

A ranch couple he identified as living over in the Broken Bit country came up the veranda steps with three youngsters and went on into the lobby. The grown-ups didn't glance at him, but the youngsters did, and he heard one of them ask, "Is that him, Pa— is that the killer marshal?"

"Hush your mouth," the woman scolded.

Soon after that Pinky Weaver quartered across Main Street and came to the Palace. "I took a ten-dollar fine from Fisher and turned him loose," the sheriff announced. "That all right with you?" In the moment Rimbow took to consider this, Weaver said, "I couldn't fine him much for just loitering."

"There was more to it than that, Pinky. Fisher was gunning for me."

"You sure?" Pinky asked, frankly surprised.

Rimbow nodded.

"Then why wasn't he charged with that?"

"No legal proof."

Weaver seemed genuinely dismayed. "Hell, I thought it was just a stunt. I figured it was your way of telling the toughs that you'd take no back talk from them at all."

"I wanted him held in jail until Monday," Rimbow said in a mildly censuring voice. "One less gun against me on Saturday night."

"You expecting bad trouble?" Weaver inquired anxiously.

"Shouldn't wonder."

The sheriff considered that in thoughtful silence before asking, "Enough trouble to need help?"

It was, Rimbow understood, a question requiring a negative answer. Pinky Weaver wasn't offering help, or even suggesting it. He was asking for a refusal that would put his frugal pride and whatever conscience he possessed at ease. Rimbow thought, *A hell of a lot of help you'd be,* and was on the point of expressing that sarcastic belief when Mrs. Weaver came along the plank walk with a shopping basket on her arm.

A fragile, seemingly undernourished woman, she asked anxiously. "Will you be home for supper on time tonight, Clarence?"

"Yes," Weaver said. "In fact I'm through for the day right now." For Rimbow's benefit, he added, "I was on duty until almost midnight yesterday."

Mrs. Weaver smiled at Rimbow. She said earnestly, with direct honesty, "I'm so pleased you took the city marshal job, Mr. Rimbow. Purely pleased. It makes it so much easier on Clarence."

"And on you?" Rimbow asked good-naturedly.

"Mercy yes! I could scarcely sleep nights for fear one of those awful shooting scrapes would end up with his getting killed."

Not Clarence, Rimbow thought. Not a sheriff who sidestepped trouble as a matter of habit. But he liked her frankness and so he said, "Don't worry about town matters, ma'am. I'll take care of them."

"Then you won't need no help Saturday night?" Weaver said eagerly.

Rimbow shook his head. "But from now on don't turn an arrested man loose until you've talked with me, regardless of the charge against him."

"I won't," Pinky promised. "I surely won't."

Rimbow watched Weaver accompany his wife toward Martin's Mercantile and wondered how so gutless a man could seem important to a wife. What was it that caused women to love a man like Pinky Weaver? The sheriff was a self-confessed coward—a prideless politician who accepted wages for a job he was afraid to do. Pinky had been a failure as a cowman, and the hardships of those bitter years had marked the woman who had shared them. Yet she worried about his welfare and feared for his safety.

Must be habit, Rimbow decided. Perhaps Pinky had been quite a man ten or fifteen years ago when she married him. Or he had seemed to be. A young man, he supposed, could make quite an impression on a young bride filled with romantic yearnings. Compared with her fragility and girlish misgivings he might have seemed a regular bull of the woods and some of that hero worship remained, regardless of the tarnish the parade of years put on her idol. If, Rimbow thought, she was that type of woman. Otherwise she'd quit him for a bigger bull of the woods or a less tarnished hero.

Lew Tiffany came out to the veranda, picking at his teeth with a toothpick. It occurred to Rimbow that this gambler also had his set routine, that he probably came from the hotel at about this same time each day.

As if resuming a conversation recently interrupted, Tiffany asked, "Have you given my proposition any more thought?"

Rimbow shook his head.

"But it would make it so much easier on you, and everybody else," Tiffany urged. "Just one night a week. Saturday night, which is considered a sort of spree day everywhere."

"What I told you still goes," Rimbow said flatly.

Tiffany frowned, and a rising resentment was revealed in his voice when he said, "I've talked to Cash Bancroft about it."

"What did he say?"

"That it was up to you."

Rimbow smiled, understanding that Bancroft had merely passed the responsibility back to where it rightfully belonged. He said, "Cash is a banker. A real good banker. I'm the city marshal."

"And you could be a real good one if you'd listen to reason," Tiffany said.

"I'd be a real good one today, if Sid Fisher's scheme hadn't misfired," Rimbow suggested.

"I had nothing to do with that," Tiffany insisted. "I'm not responsible for what goes on in Burro Alley."

Rimbow didn't see Marlene Lane until Tiffany tipped his hat to her and went quickly down the veranda steps. She allowed him to take one of the two packages she carried, but smiled at Rimbow, saying, "Good afternoon, Marshal."

She walked on along the street with Tiffany. Recalling that Pete Eggleston had said she was married, Rimbow wondered how Marlene's crippled husband liked Tiffany's attentiveness. Probably he had no choice in the matter—married or not, a saloon singer had to be nice to the man who paid her wages.

But why, Rimbow wondered, did she insist on being nice to a city marshal who had shown his dislike of her kind? Did she expect Mike O'Mara's partner to make a damned fool of himself also, or was she just bothering him for the fun of it?

There was no telling about women. They did the

damnedest things for the damnedest reasons. A man was better off not to worry himself trying to understand them. So thinking, Rimbow went into the dining room and sat down. Waiting to be served, he was amused at the way those three ranch kids gawked at him. You'd think, by God, that he was visiting royalty, or some sideshow freak.

10

Bullets Bet a Blue Chip

DEPUTY SHERIFF BEHMAN drove up to Finucane's Livery while Rimbow was smoking his after-supper cigar on the Palace veranda. Rimbow again wondered if Hawk Halliday had regained consciousness, and presently, as Behman came along the walk, thought he would soon know. The answer would be shown by Behman's destination—if Halliday had talked to the Tombstone deputy, the latter would head for the courthouse to swear out a warrant for an escaped prisoner charged with the murder of Jube Tanner. Otherwise he'd probably be interested in having supper at the Palace.

Walking with the late sunlight behind him, Behman cast a long shadow. He moved in the purposeful way of a man on an important mission; warily watching him now, Rimbow thought, *He's not coming to the hotel!*

As Behman passed on the opposite sidewalk, Jim Rimbow did some fast thinking. And now, under pressure, his thoughts were sharper and more self-searching. A few moments ago he had been undecided whether to run or stand his ground. Now he understood that by running he would be deliberately welshing on a deal that had been paid for in advance—a deal made in good faith and on which he had given his word. A man couldn't do that, and keep his pride.

He thumbed a match to flame, lit his dead cigar. It would be worth something to see Weaver's face when Pinky served the warrant.

Rimbow grinned, thinking how that would be. Pinky wouldn't force a showdown, but Behman might back him. And the Tombstone deputy looked like a man who would shoot it out. One thing, Rimbow thought, was sure—the saloon crowd would be jubilant. No matter how it ended, they could ridicule the Citizens' Committee for hiring an escaped prisoner.

Rimbow wondered if there were any way he could prove his innocence. Admitting that he was a gun-runner wouldn't help. Not now. The time for that had been when Hawk Halliday first had jumped him. He watched Behman come out of the sheriff's office, and remembered that Weaver had gone home more than an hour ago. Which meant Behman would be making tracks for Residential Avenue. Pinky's supper would be spoiled for sure; but because of what Behman's visit would do to Weaver's wife, Rimbow felt no amusement. The poor woman had said she was purely pleased because Jim Rimbow had been made city marshal.

Behman nodded to Rimbow as he came along the sidewalk. He used a handkerchief to wipe his perspiring face and muttered, "Hot day."

Rimbow watched him, not sure how this might go. Behman had no official authority in this county, but you could never tell. A gutty lawman might overreach his territory on the theory that a crime had been committed in his district. The possibility was strengthened now as Behman came up the verenda steps, using his right hand to replace the handkerchief in his pants pocket. Expecting him to draw his holstered gun Rimbow reached for his. No foreign deputy sheriff was going to arrest him, by God!

But Behman didn't draw. He asked, "They still serving supper?"

Rimbow nodded. "How's things at Spade?"

"Bad. Sam Chastain asked me to tell Pinky Weaver that his north line camp was burned down yesterday. Sam is threatening to burn Circle J in retaliation."

"A bad mess," Rimbow mused. "How is Halliday?"

"Still unconscious."

Rimbow revealed no sign of the tension those two words released. But now, as Behman went on into the lobby, a gusty sigh slid from Rimbow's lips, and because the need for physical movement was strong in him, he decided to make an early round of the town.

The sun was down and evening's first twilight softened the harsh outlines of Burro Alley. The pungent, smoky smell of the blacksmith forge was accompanied by a measured, almost musical beat of hammer on anvil. He was passing the Fandango Dancehall when a man came hurtling from the doorway and collided with him.

Acting instinctively, Rimbow jumped back and drew his gun. The man went to his hands and knees. Blood dripped from a gash in his forehead and, as he got up, Rimbow saw that a strip of hide had been peeled from the left side of his face. Recognizing the drunken hardware drummer, Rimbow asked, "What's wrong, friend?"

The man wasn't drunk now. He was painfully sober. "I got rolled in there last night," he reported solemnly. "One of those girls took eighty dollars out of my money-belt. Company funds."

"Maybe you spent it on her," Rimbow suggested. "You were pretty drunk last night."

"But I never touch company funds," the drummer insisted. "That's why I keep it in a moneybelt—so I won't make a mistake and spend it."

Rose Ducharme came to the doorway. "Don't pay no attention to him, Marshal. He's been pestering me all afternoon. Finally had to have my man throw him out."

"Does your man use brass knuckles?" Rimbow asked.

"Of course not," Rose said.

The drummer muttered, "He used 'em on me."

"You've had your fun, and you paid for it," Rose announced. "Why don't you go on about your business?"

"I can't go without that eighty dollars," he explained. "I told you I needed it to leave town—and I'm supposed to be in El Paso tomorrow. That's why I've got to have that money back."

She scoffed, "Every drunk that goes broke always claims he was rolled!"

The drummer shook his head. "Not me, ma'am. I spend my own money and that's all right. But not company funds."

Rimbow believed him. He said to Rose Ducharme, "Give him back the eighty dollars and be damned quick about it."

"But I didn't take it!" she protested. "I never touched

either him or his filthy money."

"Didn't say you did. But it happened in your place, and you're responsible. I'll have no rolling of drunks in this town—nor using brass knuckles on them. Either give him the eighty, or go to jail."

"Me—go to jail?" she demanded in disbelief.

Rimbow nodded.

"You wouldn't dare."

"Wouldn't I?" he said and grasped her wrist. "Come on."

Rose was a big woman, and a strong one. She tried to yank her arm free, and when that didn't work, she swung at him.

Rimbow blocked the blow with his left arm. He asked sharply, "You want to be handcuffed?" and realized he didn't have manacles. But the mention of them was enough for Rose Ducharme. It turned her meek at once.

She said, "All right. I'll give him the money."

The bouncer, a thin young dandy with long sideburns, had come to the doorway with two of Rose's girls. Rose turned to him and said, "Let me have eighty dollars, Ben."

When she handed the money to the drummer, the latter turned to Rimbow and said, "Thanks. Thanks very much, Marshal."

"Stay out of this alley and take the next stage out," Rimbow said.

"I will," he promised and walked hurriedly toward Main Street.

Rimbow looked Ben in the eye and said, "If I hear of you using brass knuckles again I'll put you in jail."

"But he ain't big," Rose protested. "How can he throw them out otherwise."

Rimbow shrugged. "Let him stick to pimping, then," he suggested, and walked on toward Front Street.

When the Tombstone stage departed at ten-thirty Deputy Sheriff Behman was on it, which suited Rimbow perfectly. He was smoking his second cigar of the evening in celebration of the event, when Marlene Lane came across Main Street, unaccompanied. Why, he wondered, wasn't Tiffany with her?

Marlene came directly toward the veranda; it was as if she knew he would be there, and he thought cynically, *Like I'm waiting for her* . . . but even so, he wasn't prepared for what happened now. She came up to the railing and asked smilingly, "Would you be kind enough to escort me home?"

Astonishment rifled through Jim Rimbow.

Marlene asked, "Isn't protection of citizens part of your duty as marshal?"

"Citizens, yes."

"Am I not a citizen?"

Rimbow felt like saying: *You're a goddam saloon girl* . . . but something in her warm eyes and in the smile that curved her lips kept him silent.

"I'm a taxpayer," she said.

"So?"

"Doesn't that make me eligible for protection by the city marshal?"

Rimbow tried to tell himself that this was why he got

to his feet now and said, "All right," and went down the steps. But deep inside, where a man keeps his secret and self-mocking admissions, he understood that the real prompting was in her warm eyes and smiling lips and the subtle, tempting fragrance of her. He didn't offer his arm, but she took it and walked beside him in what he supposed would be called wifely fashion—as she might walk with her husband, if her husband could walk.

When he discarded his cigar Marlene said, "You should've finished smoking it, Marshal. I like the smell of cigars."

He asked bluntly, "Why didn't Tiffany come with you tonight?"

"Because I asked him not to."

She didn't say why, and he didn't ask her.

Presently, as they passed the Alhambra where Pete Eggleston stood in the doorway, the saloonman said cheerfully, "Being city marshal has its compensations, doesn't it, friend?"

Embarrassed, Rimbow ignored him, and Marlene said, "I know how you feel about Mike O'Mara's death. He was one of the finest men I've ever met—good and full of fun, until he got drunk. Then he wasn't the same."

"A little on the wild side," Rimbow admitted. "Booze affects most men like that." And because of a sense of loyalty for Mike, he added, "It brings out the studhorse streak in them."

"I suppose. But I want you to know that Lew had no choice at all, once the trouble started. Mike forced the fight."

"Tiffany," Rimbow said, "is a yellow dog. Don't try to tell me anything else."

She didn't speak again until they passed Peppersall's Feed Store and stopped at a white picket fence in front of the little adobe house where she lived. Then she invited him into the house for a cup of coffee and astonished him by saying, "I'd like to have you meet Bill."

"But would he like it?" Rimbow demanded.

"Yes. He's leaving for Chicago in the morning to have an operation on his spine. It was Bill's idea that you should be the one to escort me, and he wants to meet the marshal who'll be responsible for my reaching home safe and sound while he's away."

Rimbow was dumbfounded. And a trifle disappointed. He had thought it was her idea—that she preferred his company to Tiffany's. The knowledge that it was her husband's wish surprised him completely. The man must be loco, along with being a cripple.

"Bill," he suggested, "probably thinks I'm an old gray-haired galoot with a goatee. Perhaps it would be better if he doesn't meet me."

Marlene laughed at him. "I've told Bill all about you," she said. "Come on in."

She reached for the gate latch, and so did he. His hand, sliding over her slim fingers, made a caressing contact and this intimacy combined with the darkness and the subtle scent of her affected him strongly.

"I told Bill you were about thirty," Marlene said, not withdrawing her hand. "Did I miss your age by much?"

"One year," he said. "I'm thirty-one."

"The same age as Bill," she said, as if this pleased her.

"But I'm not crippled," Rimbow said and pulled her against him. "Did you forget that?"

She was close now; so close that the ebb and flow of her breathing was a tangible disturbance against his chest. Her eyes were veiled shadows in the starlight, but her upturned face seemed to hold the faint half-smiling expression he had seen before—the mixture of laughter and tears, of regret and gladness, of wanting and refusing—all the deep, rich mystery of womanhood.

"No, Jim, I'm not forgetting," she murmured.

Rimbow knew then that he could kiss her, and felt a pulsing need to do it. But some tangible strand of the barrier he had built against her made him remember that these same lips had lured Mike O'Mara to his death. The moist, sweet-curving lips of this married woman. He let go of her then.

He said sharply, "Mike was drunk, but I'm sober," and walked away.

Angry now, and flustered as a man could be, he thought, *Who the hell does she think she is?*

Then, as he heard the gate close behind him, Rimbow saw an indistinct shape emerge from the alley beside Peppersall's Feed Store. Instinctively reaching for his gun, he called, "Who's there?"

A gun exploded directly ahead of him and Rimbow felt the wind-lash of a bullet past his face. He dropped to the dust as two more bullets whipped close. He had been vaguely outlined against the lamp-lit window of Marlene's house; now, lying full length, Rimbow probed the far shadows, waiting for another bloom of muzzle flame that could be used for a target. But there was none, and no sign of movement anywhere—until Marlene came running up and asked, "Are you hurt, Jim?"

Rimbow cursed, said, "Get back to the house!"

Instead of obeying, she knelt beside him in the dust and demanded, "Are you hurt?"

"No," Rimbow said and got up. "Tiffany missed all three shots."

"It wasn't Lew," Marlene said, very sure about this.

Rimbow laughed at her. "Was it his idea, having me walk you home?"

"No, Jim. And I'll tell you why I'm sure Lew had nothing to do with this shooting. When Mike O'Mara died I told Lew that if he, or any of his men, drew a gun against you, I'd quit my job."

So that was it, Rimbow thought. That was why Lew Tiffany had played the coward's role on Main Street. The big gambler had been caught between anger and greed—between the alternatives of losing an entertainer who had turned his place into a gold mine, or appearing to be afraid of Mike O'Mara's partner.

"I couldn't stand the thought of another man being killed because Mike O'Mara had kissed me," Marlene explained. Her voice was low, yet it held an urgent, pleading note. Her slim fingers were plucking at his sleeve, plucking at his emotions, too. Her voice was warm and intimate.

"So?" Rimbow mused. And then, because her smile was both a rebuke and an invitation, he took her in his arms. The flavor of her lips was like rare and intoxicating

127

wine. The scent of her hair, the sense of her yielding body, rocked all his senses as he kissed her long and hard.

A banquet to satisfy hidden hungers. . . . Poetry Pete's words were like an exultant chant in Rimbow as he peered into Marlene's upturned face. No wonder men were bewitched by this woman!

Calmly, as though there had been no interruption, Marlene whispered, "It was the only way I could make Lew let you alone."

Suddenly Pete Eggleston called from the yonder darkness, "Jim—are you all right?"

"Just dandy," Rimbow replied and released Marlene as Pete came up.

"Who fired those shots?" asked the saloonman.

"Probably some drunk from Burro Alley," Rimbow suggested. Turning to Marlene he said reluctantly, "Good night."

Her hand came out and touched his arm. "Be careful," she said, and then there was only the sound of her high heels receding into the starlit night.

11

Fast Man—Last Man

JIM RIMBOW was eating his late breakfast in the dining room when Mayor Martin came in and asked, "Any idea who shot at you last night?"

"Well, it could've been Fisher, or Rose Ducharme's man, or any of a dozen others."

The mayor was visibly upset about it. He asked, "What were you doing in that end of town?"

"Haven't you heard?" Rimbow inquired flatly.

That seemed to embarrass Martin who nodded and said, "I've heard, but it doesn't make sense to me, Jim. I never took you for a ladies' man."

"I'm not," Rimbow muttered, but the denial lacked conviction and his memory of kissing Marlene Lane was like an accusing finger. "A citizen requested protection and I gave it," he explained.

"Seems odd that a Lady Gay entertainer should request protection," Martin suggested.

That irritated Rimbow. "What's odd about it?" he demanded. "She's a woman, isn't she?"

"Yes, of course. And a very pretty woman. But I wouldn't suppose that anyone working for Lew Tiffany would require protection. He is recognized as being the top dog in the bunch that would harm a woman."

Rimbow finished his coffee and got up. He asked, "Anything else?"

"Well, I don't like the talk that's going around—about your not being here to enforce the curfew tomorrow night."

"Just talk," Rimbow told him as they walked out to the veranda. "The toughs spread that stuff to worry a star-packer."

Martin said bluntly, "It was more than talk last night. How close did those bullets come to hitting you?"

"First one was close," Rimbow admitted.

While Martin thought about that, Rimbow asked cynically, "Afraid the town will lose its five-hundred-dollar investment in me?"

Martin held up a hand and protested, "Don't talk like that, Jim. I know you're capable of doing the job, if anybody can do it. But I can't abide the thought of your being killed. It would be on my conscience."

Guessing there was more to it than that, Rimbow asked, "Has Cash Bancroft suggested taking the curfew off on Saturday night?"

"Not exactly. But he has discussed it with other members of the committee. Cash pointed out that it might be better to have an orderly town six days a week and a city marshal to keep things under control on Saturday, than to have no city marshal at all. We'd have a hard time replacing you, Jim, if anything happened."

The temptation to go along with that reasoning was strong in Rimbow. It was no hide off him if the town wanted to knuckle under to Lew Tiffany. But an inherent honesty prompted him to say, "If you back down on the Saturday night curfew there'll be no stopping them at all. Give 'em an inch and they'll take a mile. I've seen it tried before, and it never works."

"That's exactly what I said," Martin announced, visibly pleased. "I'm glad you agree with me, Jim."

"Then don't let it fret you. I've been shot at before."

"Would it do any good to have Pinky Weaver on duty with you tomorrow night?"

Rimbow shook his head. "All I want from Weaver is to keep in jail the men I arrest."

"He'll do that," Martin promised. "The Citizens' Committee will see that he does."

"*Bueno*," Rimbow said, and now, watching him walk toward the bank, felt an increased respect for Reservation's mayor.

Soon after that Rimbow saw Duke Hazelhurst drive a buggy out of Finucane's wagonyard and leave town, headed west. Where, he wondered, would Tiffany's cardsharp be going in a rented rig at this time of day? Curious about it, Rimbow sauntered over to the livery and attempted to pump information out of Finucane, but all the liveryman could tell him was that Hazelhurst rented a rig two or three times a week, was always gone for several hours and returned.

"Maybe," Rimbow suggested, "he wants to get the stink of this town out of his nostrils occasionally." He saw Sid Fisher come out of Burro Alley with Rose Ducharme's bouncer, and asked, "Who's that with Fisher?"

"Ben Moselle," Monk said. "He's the main stud at the Fandango."

Rimbow watched them cross Main Street, Sid's derby perched high because of the bandage around his head. They made a pair, those two—a slick-dressed pair of parasites.

As they went into the Kansas Cafe, Finucane asked, "Do ye think one of thim Fancy Dans done the shootin' last night?"

Rimbow nodded.

"Which one?"

"Well, I suppose Fisher had the most reason to want revenge," Rimbow said, thinking this out as he spoke. "But Moselle is the right breed of cat, also."

"He is that. If 'twas me wearin' the star I'd throw thim both in jail on suspicion. That'd make two ye wouldn't have to worry about Saturday night."

"Maybe so," Rimbow agreed.

As he reached for his Durham sack, Monk plucked a cigar from his vest pocket. "Have a real smoke, Jim. It will settle your nerves."

Accepting the cigar and lighting it, Rimbow said, "That pair won't be hard to handle. Not in daylight."

Rimbow quartered across Main Street, walking in leisurely fashion and pausing a moment in the doorway of the saddle shop to pass a few words with Fritz Elmendorf. Two riders trotted into town from the west. As they turned in at Finucane's Livery and dismounted, Rimbow observed Winchesters in their saddle scabbards. He was standing at the west corner of the Kansas Cafe smoking the last of his cigar when the two men came along the opposite sidewalk. One of them, a tall, roan-faced man, he identified as Red Nedrow whom he had seen in Abilene; the other was the dry-gulcher who had freed him from a dead horse, Joe Bodine.

Rimbow watched them go into the barbershop. The cafe's screen door opened and Fisher and Moselle came out. Fisher turned to say, "See you later, Goldie, girl."

They were on the sidewalk when Rimbow said sharply, "You're under arrest."

The two men eyed him in astonishment, Moselle demanding, "What for?"

"Loitering," Rimbow said. "Turn around and walk to the sheriff's office."

"You can't arrest us for loitering!" Fisher protested.

Rimbow drew his gun. "I already have," he said. "Start walking."

Moselle obeyed at once, but Fisher balked, and now a blonde waitress called from the cafe doorway, "They weren't loitering, Marshal. They were eating breakfast."

Ignoring her, Rimbow stepped close to Fisher, jabbing with his gun. That convinced Sid. He joined Moselle, the two of them walking side by side in the stiff, resentful way of men hating each step they took. When they came abreast of the Mercantile doorway Sid Fisher shouted, "Mayor Martin!"

Amused at this, Rimbow allowed them to stop while the mayor came out, listened patiently while Fisher announced, "Your city marshal has arrested us for loitering. In broad daylight, by God!"

Mayor Martin peered at Rimbow and asked, "Is that the charge against them, Jim?"

Rimbow nodded. "Also suspicion of firing at me last night."

"Very well," Martin said and went back into his store.

Rimbow commanded, "Move on—you're obstructing the sidewalk," and identified Billy Dial in the gathering crowd of curious spectators.

When Rimbow turned his prisoners over to Sheriff Weaver he said, "No fine on these, Pinky. Just keep 'em in jail."

Weaver nodded his understanding. As he relieved the two men of their weapons, Rimbow asked, "How many cells in your jail?"

"Five, each with two bunks. You expecting more arrests?"

Rimbow shrugged. "Depends on how things go tomorrow night."

Afterward, sitting on the Palace veranda, he saw Duke Hazelhurst drive into town from the west. Still wondering where the cardsharp had been, Rimbow watched him turn the rig over to Finucane and then come along the street. It occurred to Rimbow that he had never seen Duke less than well-dressed, or needing a shave, or a bath. In a country where men were generally careless about such things, Duke Hazelhurst made a religion of fastidiousness.

Duke waited for a freight wagon to pass in front of the hotel, then crossed the street and came up the veranda steps. "Hot day," he said, and took the chair next to Rimbow.

"Cooler up on the mesa?" Rimbow inquired.

"Some."

Hazelhurst took a cigar from his vest pocket and used a pearl-handled knife to clip its end. It was past four o'clock now, and a time when he would ordinarily be at the Lady Gay.

Rimbow was wondering about this when Duke said, "I've got a message for you." He took a gold-plated badge from his pocket and handed it to Rimbow. "From Hawk Halliday."

Rimbow saw the lettering on the badge: DEPUTY UNITED STATES MARSHAL.

"How come?" he asked.

"Hawk wants you to arrest three men the first chance you get."

Rimbow put the badge in his pocket. This, he thought amazedly, was Hawk's method of making a deal—a way of helping his friend Sam Chastain even though bedfast with bullet wounds. "Three Jardine riders?"

"Yes. Red Nedrow, Zig Chisum and Kid Antrim," Hazelhurst said. "They're wanted for mail robbery in Texas."

A cynical smile quirked Rimbow's lips as he said, "And for fighting against Spade."

Hazelhurst shrugged. He eyed Rimbow for a moment as if seeking a clue to something that puzzled him. "I hear you were riding with Halliday at the time he got ambushed."

"Yes?"

"And that you brought the news to Spade."

"Well, what of it?" Rimbow inquired.

Hazelhurst knocked dead ash from his cigar and relit it before saying, "Johnny Behman told me yesterday that

Halliday was trailing a murderer north from Tanner's Trading Post."

"So?"

"Behman seemed to think he had brought the news to Reservation—that no one here knew about the murder."

Keeping a tight check on the apprehension that rose in him now, Rimbow asked calmly, "Is that important?"

Hazelhurst studied him for another moment before giving his attention to the cigar again. Finally he said, "I guess not."

Eager to divert the trend of conversation, Rimbow asked, "How is Hawk feeling?"

"Well, he regained consciousness this morning. His head wound seems to be responding to treatment. But he lost a considerable amount of blood and he will be laid up with a broken leg for some time."

"Did he give you any other message for me?"

Hazelhurst shook his head.

Rimbow waited for him to explain or give some reason for the visit to Spade. How was it that a cardsharp called on a wounded deputy U. S. marshal?

Finally Rimbow said, not wanting to put the question directly, "The man must make a habit of calling on wounded lawmen, regardless of how far he has to travel."

That seemed to embarrass Hazelhurst. He said mildly, "That's none of your business," and rose from the chair.

Watching him walk toward the Lady Gay, Rimbow was both puzzled and pleased. Hawk Halliday had regained consciousness but he hadn't told about the prisoner he was bringing to jail. Instead, the old man had offered a deal.

Then it occurred to him that one of the men Halliday wanted was in town—Red Nedrow. A thin smile quirked his lips. He crossed the street and looked into the barber-shop. Nedrow and Bodine had left. Nor were they in the Kansas Cafe where the blonde waitress demanded, "Why are you always picking on Sid Fisher?"

"My business, and none of yours," Rimbow said.

"It is so my business," Goldie insisted. "Sid is my boy friend!" As Rimbow turned back to the sidewalk she came out and said angrily, "I offered to go his bail but they said you wanted him kept in a cell."

When Rimbow still ignored her, she shouted, "You big coward—you're afraid of him!"

Three railroad men, loafing in front of the restaurant, heard that accusation, and one of them said approvingly, "Tell him off, gal—tell him off."

There was frank amusement on the faces of other men as Rimbow walked along the street, and he thought the story would be all over town within an hour.

Shrugging off his irritation, Rimbow walked into the Lady Gay. He identified Joe Bodine among the dozen men at the bar, but failed to find Red Nedrow until he shifted his gaze to the gambling layouts—then he saw Nedrow at the poker table where Duke Hazelhurst was dealing stud to four players.

Bodine saw him in the backbar mirror. The chunky rider turned, stared at the star on his vest and then came up to him, demanding, "How come you got a badge, friend?"

"Hired on as city marshal," Rimbow said.

Bodine studied him in stunned silence for a moment. Then a grin rutted his beefy cheeks and he said, "That makes it perfect, by grab—you and Pinky Weaver. Come and have a drink with me."

Rimbow shook his head. Speaking softly now, he said, "I made you a promise, and I'll keep it. But don't get in my way."

"What you mean by that?"

"What I said—don't get in my way."

He walked over to the poker table, watched Nedrow make a fifty-dollar bet on a bluff and lose it. Then, as Hazelhurst pushed the pot to the winner, Rimbow said, "Hello, Red."

Nedrow glanced up at him. Angered at losing the big pot, he snapped, "So you're toting a tin badge again, Rimbow."

"Not tin," Rimbow disagreed, and opened the palm of his left hand, revealing the U. S. marshal's badge. "Gold."

Nedrow's cheeks tightened. His bleached blue eyes darted from the badge to Rimbow's gun and he demanded, "Why you showing it to me?"

"Federal warrant," Rimbow said. "Get up."

He was aware of a hush settling over the big room. Hazelhurst and the other three players sat motionless— Bodine, watching him from the bar, poised a glass of whiskey in his right hand.

"Get up," Rimbow ordered.

Red pushed back his chair. He asked, "You arresting me?"

Rimbow nodded, saw Red's eyes tighten and guessed

how this was going to be—Nedrow would grab as he got up.

Sure knowledge rifling through him, Rimbow drew his gun and saw Red's right hand dart to holster. Rimbow fired a split second before Nedrow, whose bullet splintered the table top. As the redhead fell backward, taking the chair with him, Rimbow shifted his gaze to Bodine.

The beefy-faced rider still held the whiskey glass—now, under the impact of Rimbow's questioning eyes he said urgently, "I'm out of it, friend."

"Go get Doc Carter," Rimbow ordered.

Bodine turned from the bar, gulping his drink and discarding the glass. He went outside.

Hazelhurst had knelt beside Nedrow. He looked up and announced, "I think this one is arrested permanently, Jim."

"Shouldn't wonder," Rimbow said and, as Lew Tiffany elbowed his way through the ring of spectators, asked, "Will you have a couple of your men tote him to the jail?"

The saloonman glanced at Nedrow's sprawled body. He said, "You've bought yourself some real trouble." Then he said to Billy Dial, "Get this out of here. It's bad for business."

12

Back-shooter's Gold

THE NEWS of Red Nedrow's shooting traveled fast. Within a few minutes it was being told along Main Street and in Burro Alley. The alley received the report with joyful anticipation, Blacky Pratt predicting, "Now he's in trouble for sure. That Circle J bunch will take this town apart."

At dusk Jim Rimbow sat on the hotel veranda and waited for Doctor Carter to return from the jail. It seemed unlikely that a man would survive a .45 caliber bullet fired at point-blank range, yet Doc wouldn't remain long with a dead man. Which must mean that Nedrow was still alive.

Duke Hazelhurst came from the lobby and stood for a moment, as if to make sure that no one else was within earshot. Then he said quietly, "One down, two to go." The silence rode on for a long moment before he added: "Bodine left town soon afterwards, Jim. He rode west."

"So?"

Hazelhurst studied this lanky lawman who sat seemingly relaxed and unconcerned. "Don't you understand what that means? Don't you know what's going to happen

140

when those toughs hear that a Circle J rider has been shot?"

"You think they'll break down and cry?" Rimbow asked, unconcerned.

Hazelhurst said thoughtfully, "I'd hate to be in your boots when that bunch arrives in town."

The gambler went down the steps and walked toward the Lady Gay Saloon in leisurely fashion. Watching him, Rimbow wondered what circumstance in the past could have spawned a friendship between him and Halliday. Neither man was given to making easy alliances—each was aloof and, in his way, arrogant. Yet Hazelhurst had brought Halliday's badge to town in what was probably the oddest deal ever offered an escaped prisoner.

It didn't add up.

But Rimbow's puzzlement on that score was a trifling thing compared to the announcement Doctor Carter made when he came to the veranda and said, "Nedrow had the wind knocked out of him, and has a broken rib. But that's all. He had his shirt off when I arrived. There was a bad bruise just below his heart and he had guzzled most of a pint of whiskey to kill the pain the rib was giving him. Bullet must've been fired at an angle, but I still don't understand it."

"Angle, hell," Rimbow disagreed. "It was head-on, and no farther than six or eight feet at most."

"Perhaps he turned just as the bullet struck," the medico suggested. Then he asked wonderingly, "Are you disappointed because the man didn't die?"

Rimbow stared at him.

"No, but I can't afford to use bullets that bounce.

Peace officer gets a reputation for only bruising his targets he'll have every two-bit badman in the country shooting at him. A man had better not draw at all unless he shoots to kill."

The physician said with mild censure, "I suppose a city marshal has to be callous about taking human life," and walked on along the darkening street.

Callous? Just because he outdrew a Texas bandit.

That, Rimbow supposed, was what they were all thinking, all the respectable ones who didn't know how it was to face a shoot-out. But men like Red Nedrow knew; to them a star-packer was either fast or slow. The wild ones had no respect for a slow man, or mercy for a fast one.

But how had Nedrow escaped with only a broken rib?

Abruptly then Rimbow thought of something else—something that might explain a great deal. With an increasing sense of anticipation prodding him he walked toward the jail. Doc Carter might be right about Nedrow turning slightly as he drew his gun, but it took more than that to deflect a bullet.

The jailer gave Rimbow the ring of cell keys and asked sourly, "You seen the sheriff this evenin'?"

Rimbow shook his head and stepped into the corridor that ran back, from the sheriff's office.

"That's Pinky Weaver for you," the jailer complained. "Never around when things happen."

One bracket-lamp gave the jail a dim illumination. Rimbow identified the obscure faces of Moselle and Fisher in the first cell. The next two were vacant, then he came to No. 4, where Nedrow lay on his bunk. Rimbow unlocked the barred gate and stepped inside with that pulse-throbbing anticipation in him.

"What you want?" the redhead inquired, looking up sullenly.

"Curious about your wound," Rimbow said. "Take off your shirt."

Red sat up. "I got a broken rib, and it hurts like hell." His voice was thick and his breath whiskey-tainted. "Leave me be."

Rimbow reached out and grasped Nedrow's cotton shirt at the collar and ripped it open, revealing a leather vest beneath it.

"What the hell?" Red protested.

"Nedrow—spell it backwards and it comes out Worden," Rimbow said softly. "Give me the vest."

"No," Red muttered. "Leave me be."

All the pent-up resentment of the past few days flamed high and hot in Rimbow now. Here was the renegade who had robbed him and for whose crime he had worn handcuffs. He said rankly, "You back-shooting bastard!"

Then he slugged him.

Red loosed a wooshing sigh. He lay unmoving as Rimbow stripped off the leather vest and put it on himself. The garment was heavy, but the weight of it was pleasing. He locked the cell gate and went along the corridor. Most of the gold eagles, he believed, were still packed tightly in its lining.

Sid Fisher yelled, "What's the idea of slugging a man who's got a broken rib?"

As Rimbow walked on without speaking, Ben Moselle

called, "You'll get your needings some night, right in the gut!"

Rimbow paid them no heed. In him was the exhilaration of a man privileged to clear himself of a murder charge, and in so doing he had regained possession of the most money he'd ever owned. He grinned sourly at the coincidence of the vest's having saved both his life and Nedrow's—the only bullet proof vest in Apache Basin, he thought.

Handing the key ring to the jailer, Rimbow said pleasantly, "Don't let Nedrow break out on you. He's an important federal prisoner."

"Federal?"

"U. S. Marshal's office."

"What's he wanted for?"

"Train robbery in Texas," Rimbow said. "Keep a close watch on him."

Feeling better than he had felt since the day he had crossed the Border for the last time, Rimbow walked to the Alhambra Saloon and announced, "Drinks are on me."

There were five customers at the bar; they stared at the city marshal in disbelief, and Poetry Pete demanded, "Are you drunk?"

Rimbow grinned at him. "Set them up," he said, "and bring mine to your room."

Going into Pete's living quarters at the rear of the saloon he closed the door and took off the leather vest. There was a rip in back that had been mended, and another through the bottom of the left pocket. Observing a considerable bulge below the pocket he understood that Nedrow had craftily crammed double-eagles into the lower lining so they wouldn't spill from the bullet-torn opening.

Rimbow used a knife on the lining and was dumping gold pieces onto the bed when Pete came in with two glasses. The saloonman looked at the gold and exclaimed, "God A'mighty—have you robbed the bank!"

Briefly then, while they had their drink, Rimbow told him what had happened at Tanner's Trading Post. "But I've got no legal proof, just my word. So keep it a secret, Pete."

A few of the gold pieces were misshapen, three of them bent almost double.

"Fourteen hundred and eighty dollars—and I worked damn hard for this money," Rimbow mused. "When you close up tonight put it in your safe."

"You're practically wealthy," Eggleston suggested, admiring the stacked gold eagles.

"Half goes to Mike's folks in Ohio," Rimbow said, and with the thought that Mike wasn't here to celebrate this windfall, the exhilaration faded from him.

It was an odd thing. These gold pieces, which had seemed so valuable the day he had ridden into Tanner's Trading Post, were less important now than the fact he had found Worden. With Mike O'Mara to share them—to share the satisfaction and the benefit—it would have been different.

Sensing his regret, Eggleston said, "Not your fault, Jim."

"A hell of a thing," Rimbow muttered, covering the gold with a blanket. "I'll have to ride to the ranch Monday and get the mailing address of Mike's folks."

As they went out to the barroom, Pete said, "Have a drink on me, Jim."

Rimbow shook his head. "Got to make my rounds."

He was at the doorway when Pinky Weaver turned in from the sidewalk, his face flushed and an urgency in his voice as he announced, "Riley Jardine came to town and is raising hell about Red Nedrow's arrest!"

"So?"

"He's at the jail with Mayor Martin and Cash Bancroft. He says his men are threatening to free Nedrow unless he's turned loose."

Accompanying Weaver along the street, Rimbow asked, "What does Martin say?"

"That it's up to you. But Cash Bancroft says we should do like Riley says."

"Bankers," Rimbow muttered, smearing the word with contempt.

"Those Circle J riders mean business, Jim. If they go in after Nedrow somebody'll get hurt sure as hell."

"Your worry," Rimbow said flatly. "I arrest them. It's up to the sheriff to hang onto them. Wasn't that our agreement?"

Weaver nodded. "But I didn't suppose it'd be Circle J men. Not them Texas guns."

"I'm one myself," Rimbow said, and started crossing to the jail.

Martin, Bancroft and Jardine were waiting in the sheriff's office with the sour-faced jailer. As Rimbow stepped inside, Jardine demanded, "What's this I hear about your having a federal warrant for Red Nedrow?"

"You heard right."

"Let's see the warrant."

Rimbow glanced at Martin and Bancroft, observing the gravity of their frowning faces, and guessing what their attitude would be. "Hawk Halliday has the warrant. He sent word in to me."

"Can you prove that," Jardine inquired sarcastically, "or are we supposed to just take your word for it?"

Resenting the man's arrogance, Rimbow asked, "Are you calling me a liar?"

They eyed one another in silence for a tight interval before Jardine said, "No. But this is an important thing and you should have some proof."

"I have," Rimbow said and took Hawk's badge from his pocket. "Halliday sent this to me."

Cash Bancroft said, "That's no proof you have a warrant."

And Mayor Martin asked, "Was it necessary for you to arrest Nedrow simply because Halliday requested it?"

"Yes," Rimbow said. Thinking of the lawman's odd deal and what it had meant to him, he added, "Damned necessary."

"I don't see why," Jardine announced. "You're a local officer—a city marshal. There might have been some excuse if Halliday had asked Sheriff Weaver to make the arrest. He's a county officer."

Rimbow grinned at him. "Has Pinky ever arrested a Circle J man?"

"To hell with that kind of talk. I say you're a local officer paid for local law enforcement. Red did nothing today that warranted his arrest."

147

"So?" Rimbow prompted.

"So you turn him loose at once!" Jardine snapped.

Rimbow shook his head. "I don't run this jail."

Mayor Martin nodded agreement. "That was the understanding," he said, a worried man wanting to be fair. "We agreed to keep in jail any man you arrested."

"And Rimbow has no responsibility, once a man's in jail?" Bancroft asked.

Rimbow put in, "That's up to the sheriff. If he wants my help all he has to do is ask for it."

Jardine turned to Martin and said in a worried, almost desperate way, "John, I can't stop my men from doing what they intend to do. They wanted to ride up here and take the jail, first off. But I asked them to give me two hours—until midnight. Time enough to reason with you and Pinky. I don't say Red Nedrow is any angel. But why should there be a big shootout just because your city marshal happens to be a friend of Hawk Halliday who happens to be a friend of Sam Chastain? That's who's behind this mess—a Castain trick to take men off my payroll!"

"Shouldn't wonder," Martin admitted. Turning to Rimbow, he asked, "Are you willing to have Pinky turn Nedrow loose?"

"No."

"Suppose he does, anyway?" asked Cash Bancroft.

"He won't, unless John tells him to," Rimbow said quietly. "In that case I'm making no more arrests. This job is tough enough as it is. Once you start turning arrested men loose a city marshal might as well quit."

"By God, Rimbow—you don't understand what'll happen!" Jardine shouted, anger staining his face. "Why can't you listen to reason?"

"Reason?" Rimbow inquired. "Or bald-faced stuff?" Then, because a kindred anger was burning in him, he said, "Do the rest of your damned reasoning with men who like it," and walked out of the jail office.

13

Hour of Decision

STARTING HIS ten o'clock round late, Rimbow walked slowly past the Lady Gay Saloon. The unintelligible gibberish of many voices conversing in the high pitch of whiskey buoyancy came from the open doorway; it merged with the methodical beat of a piano and the continuing laughter of men venting their ribald humor. Giving his strict attention to the hitchrack, Rimbow observed five horses wearing Circle J brands. That, he assumed, meant Joe Bodine, Kid Antrim and Zig Chisum were in the saloon awaiting the outcome of Jardine's pressure play at the jail office.

Rimbow was past the saloon when he met Monk Finucane and Fred Peppersall walking east and seeming in a hurry.

"That meeting at the jail still going on?" Peppersall asked.

When Rimbow nodded, Finucane asked, "Why ain't you at it, Jim?"

"Told them what I thought, which didn't take long," Rimbow said and walked on, turning into Burro Alley.

Finucane, he supposed, had been sent to get Peppersall. The liveryman would probably vote to keep Nedrow in jail, come hell or high water, but Rimbow wasn't optimistic about Peppersall.

As he came abreast of the Shamrock Saloon doorway where Tay Daecy stood with another man, Daecy said, "Marshal, shake hands with Frank Murdock, who'd like a word with ye."

Wondering about this, Rimbow asked, "Construction boss for the railroad, aren't you?"

The broad-shouldered, elderly Murdock nodded. "I've been hunting bridge timbers and ties for two weeks. Found a good stand of timber I understood belonged to Riley Jardine, on a mortgage deal. But today Cash Bancroft told me it's yours."

"On my place in the Owl Hoots?"

Murdock nodded. "All we want is the big stuff. I'll pay top price and furnish an accurate report of what we take out."

"Any idea what it will come to, in dollars?" Rimbow inquired.

"Well, upwards of three thousand would be my guess."

Three thousand dollars—and he would still own the land. No wonder Riley Jardine had loaned Mike five hundred on his half of the place, and been so eager to buy the rest of it!

"You've made a deal," Rimbow said.

Afterward, when the contract had been signed at the railroad depot, Rimbow walked along Front Street and thought that it was odd how luck went with a man—for a time it had seemed as if his had run out; now it seemed he couldn't stop being lucky.

When he got back to the sheriff's office, the jailer sat alone with his feet propped on Pinky's desk. Pausing at the doorway, Rimbow asked, "You still got Nedrow?"

The man nodded. "But I'm getting out of here pronto at midnight. What happens after that is no concern of mine."

"Another deputy coming on duty at twelve?" Rimbow inquired.

The jailer shook his head. "We lock this office from midnight to six in the morning."

So that's it, Rimbow thought. Without any jailer on duty it would be a simple matter to force the sheriff's office door, obtain the cell keys and free Red Nedrow. No shooting. No disturbance. Just a nice peaceful compromise between a worried mayor and the boss of a warrior ranch crew. So simple a compromise that Rimbow wondered why he hadn't suspected matters would turn out like this. To back down was the usual practice of citizens' committees in the clutch. Regardless of their fine resolutions about strict law enforcement they invariably weaseled in a showdown.

Rimbow shrugged and walked on to the Palace veranda. It was no business of his, he reflected. In fact this setup made things easy for him. He had arrested Nedrow, making good on at least part of his debt to Halliday. There would be no point in arresting the other two if they couldn't be kept in jail. Thinking ahead to how it would be at midnight, Rimbow eased back in his chair, wholly relaxed. He could be on Front Street at that time, which was his normal procedure; when he finished the night's final round Jardine's bunch would have freed Nedrow and left town.

It was almost eleven o'clock now. Time for Marlene Lane to be going home. He wondered if she would come across the street alone.

She did. And because there was an eagerness in him that he couldn't control, Rimbow went down the steps to meet her, hat in hand.

"I wondered if you'd be here," she said, and smiled up at him.

He stood a moment savoring the loveliness of her face, the utter grace of her being, and despite himself blurted, "I wish you weren't married, Marlene."

His frankness seemed to please her. "Do you, Jim?" she asked. "Do you really?" And when Rimbow nodded, she murmured, "I'm glad."

Her admission stirred a rankling resentment in him, but he offered his arm and walked along a dark street beside her.

"Bill left on the morning train," Marlene said in the tranquil voice of a woman reporting a pleasant occurrence. "He had to ride in a caboose, but it will be better than a stage. Not so many bumps to give him misery."

"I hope the operation is a success," Rimbod offered.

"Oh, I'm sure it will be. And it will mean so much to Bill. Not just physically, but mentally. He hates having me sing in a saloon."

Rimbow could understand that. Any man worth his salt wouldn't want his wife entertaining a bunch of damned drunks, night after night.

"Are you going to quit Tiffany?" he asked.

Marlene shook her head. "I've saved only enough money to pay for half the hospital and surgical expenses. I'll have to keep working until Bill is able to get a job, and that may be quite a while."

They were at the picket fence now, and she asked, "Have you time for a cup of coffee?"

Rimbow stood there with her at the gate, not sure about this woman who sang in a saloon; sweet-smelling wife of a cripple. *A fine, gracious young woman,* Pete Eggleston had called her. *Not a wanton hussy.* . . . But now she was inviting him into her house where they would be alone . . . and . . .

"A penny for your thoughts," Marlene offered teasingly.

"Just wondering, is all."

"If you have time for a cup of coffee?"

Rimbow shook his head.

"About me?"

"Yes."

That pleased her for she grasped his right arm with both hands and said, "Oh, Jim, you're so sweet."

"Sweet?" he echoed, wholly astonished.

Marlene nodded and smiled up at him and said softly, "You're as I hoped you would be. A man with principle. A man with some respect for women."

Rimbow laughed at her. Whom did she think she was funning?

A tough, taunting amusement was in his voice as he said, "Me—respect for women?" And then, because his denial seemed to have no effect; because she still clung to his arm he added sarcastically: "Respect for a saloon singer?" He turned abruptly and walked away.

154

Marlene called softly, "Good night, Jim."

"Good night!" he answered, and kept going. By God she was an odd one.

How was a man to figure such a woman? Talking about an absent husband one minute and then inviting a man into her house like a Burro Alley whore. She seemed so damned refined; so wholesome and ladylike you'd think she had never seen the inside of a saloon. That, he supposed, was what appealed to Tiffany's customers—the contrast between what she was and what she appeared to be. And that loco talk about his being a man of principle. A respecter of women.

Yet, even believing that she had tried simply to flatter him, he couldn't discard the memory of her star-lit face, smiling calmly, and the way she had said good night, as if what he had told her made no difference at all.

At eleven-twenty Duke Hazelhurst pushed a pot toward Kid Antrim and then signaled to Billy Dial. When Billy came to the poker table Duke handed him the deck of cards and said, "I'm going to get a cup of coffee."

"Headache?" Billy asked, sitting down and riffling the cards in expert fashion.

Hazelhurst nodded, and Zig Chisum said amusedly, "If you see that damned city marshal tell him we'll be over to get Red right after midnight."

Ignoring the request, Duke made his leisurely way to the street and glanced at the Palace veranda. Seeing no sign of Rimbow there, he went to the sheriff's office and spoke briefly with the jailer, then walked back toward the Palace and finally observed Rimbow going up the veranda steps.

Presently, as Hazelhurst took a chair beside the city marshal, he said, "Jailer tells me there'll be nobody on duty after midnight."

Rimbow nodded.

"Well, I happen to know that Antrim, Chisum and Bodine intend to take Nedrow out of there."

"How about Jardine? Won't he join the fun also?"

"I think he went home, but maybe not. He came into the Lady Gay half an hour or so ago. He told his men that there was nothing more he could do and was going home. Then he said that the jail office closed at midnight—a sly way of telling them there'd be no opposition."

Surprised that this gambler should be an informer, Rimbow asked, "Make any difference to you if Nedrow gets out?"

"Yes."

"Secret?"

Hazelhurst considered that for a moment. Then he said, "I don't like to admit this, but it so happens that I am courting Eve Chastain. Secretly. We meet two or three times a week up on the mesa. That's how I came by Halliday's badge. Eve gave it to me, along with the message. Her father thinks she came all the way to town, but she had a prior engagement to meet me up there. Does all this seem rather complicated to you, Jim?"

"No, but a little surprising."

Hazelhurst nodded. "I should never have let myself get involved with so fine a girl. I've suggested breaking it off, but Eve insists that we—well, that we have a right to each other."

Rimbow's face twisted in familiar emotion—he was both amused and bitter. "But you're not sure of any such right—and so you would let me die for a woman's whim."

The gambler studied him moodily. Then he said, "I've asked you one thing only. Are you going to let them take Nedrow out of jail?"

Rimbow shrugged. "It's Weaver's responsibility. Not mine."

"But you're the one who could stop them. You know that, and so does everyone else. If you let them get away with this you'll never be able to enforce a curfew tomorrow night."

"So?"

"It is your choice, Jim, not Eve Chastain's or mine. She brought me a message, and I passed it to you. Make your own decision." Duke got up and walked over to the veranda steps. "Zig Chisum doesn't think you've got any self-respect. He said to tell the damned city marshal they'd be over to get Nedrow right after midnight."

Duke was on the sidewalk when Rimbow said rankly, "Tell Chisum if it's a fight he wants, he can always call the place and time."

Hazelhurst turned and smiled back at Rimbow. He said, "Be glad to, Jim," and went on across the street.

14

Blood of a Lawdog

Jim Rimbow came to the sheriff's office door, took a final drag on his smoke and flipped it into the street. At this hour there was only one nearby light—in the Wells Fargo stage office, a company rule to discourage burglars.

"What you want?" the jailer inquired.

Not looking at him, Rimbow said, "You can go home now."

The lights were going out at the Lady Gay and a large crowd of customers milled about in front of the place. Those customers weren't dispersing as they usually did. Evidently Hazelhurst had delivered his message to Zig Chisum.

The jailer came to the doorway and asked, "You taking over the office?"

Rimbow nodded.

The man peered at him as if wholly puzzled. "I thought you said it was Pinky Weaver's worry."

"It is," Rimbow said. "But worry ain't enough."

The jailer continued to study him. He said, "Don't be a damned fool, mister. Pinky owes his election to Riley

158

Jardine, and the merchants of this town like Jardine's trade. They aren't taking sides in the Circle J and Spade ruckus. Why should you?"

The thought came to Rimbow that this man was trying to do him a favor; that he was offering counsel to keep a city marshal from taking a needless risk. Contemplating the jailer's grave, middle-aged face, Rimbow asked, "What's your name?"

"Sam Tisdale."

"Well, I'm much obliged for your advice, Sam. And I'm not saying it's not sound. But I'm taking over here, regardless."

Tisdale shrugged, not understanding this, but not much caring. "It's all yours," he muttered, and crossing the street, headed toward Residential Avenue.

A respectable married man, Rimbow supposed, with a respectable wife waiting for him. Maybe even a good wife. There'd be a midnight snack, perhaps, and then Sam and his wife would go to bed.

Rimbow glanced along the dark street, observing no nearby traffic, then walked into the jail corridor and tried the gate of Nedrow's cell. It was locked, and Nedrow seemed to be asleep on his bunk. Sid Fisher mumbled something to Moselle as Rimbow went back to the office. There was a Winchester on a rack above Pinky's desk. Presently, searching the desk drawers, he found a box of cartridges and a loaded revolver, which he put on top of the desk, alongside the Winchester.

Satisfied, Rimbow turned out the light. It must be past twelve o'clock, he thought, and wondered why Jardine's toughs hadn't already knocked on the door.

It shouldn't have taken long for them to snatch Winchesters from saddle scabbards and walk over here, even if they were drunk. But they would arrive eventually.

There had been a time when the pressure of waiting for a showdown like this would have flustered him, would have tangled his thinking and tightened his muscles. Now he waited with an almost fatalistic calm, knowing himself to be as deadly as any who might be mustered against him.

At one point he realized that his preparations hadn't been complete—he hadn't checked the jail's rear door, had assumed that the deputy's lockup was complete. He got up and was crossing the dark office when a man called from outside, "You in there, Rimbow?"

"Yes."

"Open the door."

Another man warned, "Come out, or we'll smoke you out!"

Rimbow moved behind Weaver's high roll-top desk and called tauntingly, "Start smoking."

There was a moment of consultation out front, then a voice that sounded like Joe Bodine's called, "Don't be a damn fool, Rimbow."

"I warned you once to keep out of my way," Rimbow announced. "As of right now you're my meat, Bodine."

A gunshot punctuated the threat, the bullet shattering glass in the front window.

Now it starts, Rimbow thought, and felt a familiar sense of fatalistic relief.

Another slug came through the window at an angle and ricocheted noisily off a cell bar.

Sid Fisher yelled, "Close the corridor door, Rimbow!"

Rimbow laughed at him, thinking it would be poetic justice if a stray bullet cut down one of his prisoners.

There were five shots now, one right after the other, and all plunking into the door. Two of the bullets clanged off metal, and Rimbow understood that they were being aimed at the lock in an effort to smash it. Easing around to the far side of the shattered window, he aimed low and fired. Sometimes a ricocheting slug was a better persuader than a direct hit. It might give him the time he needed to check the back door.

Moving fast, he crossed the office and was at the corridor opening when he felt a draft of cool air. For a split second the significance of it didn't register; then, with a sickening surety he realized the back door was open.

Stepping to the wall, Rimbow dropped to one knee and peered into the corridor, seeking a target. It was pitch dark back there. He heard no sound of movement, and now felt no draft. The door was shut again.

The shots had sounded sharp and loud across the quiet town. They aroused a great many people, most of whom knew nothing about an impending jail break.

Marlene Lane was having her usual midnight snack when she heard the first shot. Going quickly to the doorway she stood there listening, and hoping there wouldn't be another, and yet was apprehensive because there wasn't another shot, thinking *That might have killed Jim Rimbow!*

Mayor Martin sat up in bed at his Residential Avenue home, listened to the continued firing and muttered, "Now what?" Against his wife's protests, he began to dress. "I'll have to go find out."

His wife said, not without bitterness, "Why not let your high-priced city marshal look after it."

Pinky Weaver didn't fully wake up until he was tucking his shirt tail into his pants. "Sounds like real trouble," he said. "I'd better go take a look."

"But the town is his worry, isn't it," Ida Weaver protested. "They chose him—you were elected county officer—"

Weaver's face showed more gravity than his wife had ever seen and his voice held an odd note of self-reproach as he said, "I think it's at the jail, which means it's my worry." He thought for a moment, puzzled that it should matter, and then said firmly, "The jail's county."

He buckled on his gunbelt, put on his hat and went out so hurriedly that the screen door banged behind him.

Rimbow was still crouched beside the corridor doorway when another barrage of continued firing came from out front, smashing the lock. The door swung open. Rimbow pushed the heavy desk against it.

Footsteps came from the passageway. Rimbow whirled and fired a random shot and ducked aside.

Pinky Weaver's voice implored frantically, "Don't shoot, Jim—it's me!" Weaver came on into the office and asked nervously, "Where you at, Jim?"

"Here," Rimbow directed and, as the sheriff's shape

came through the smoke-tainted darkness, asked with a hint of doubt, "Shooting disturb your sleep?"

It was an odd thing, and it gave Rimbow pause. Neither of them had any exact knowledge of the other's facial expressions, yet they both chuckled simultaneously.

Pinky said, "I don't cotton to city marshals taking over my office just like they owned it."

"Hell of a note," Rimbow agreed.

Two more bullets came through the shattered window and clanged off metal in the corridor.

"Shut that damn door before you get us killed!" Sid Fisher screeched. "Them slugs are going every which way!"

As if in reply to that there was a concentrated firing from the outside—when it died down, Rimbow asked, "Where's your handcuffs, Pinky?"

"On my belt. Want 'em?"

"Yes," Rimbow said. "Might arrest a man, maybe two men if I'm lucky."

"How so?" Weaver asked.

"Just give me the backdoor key and don't ask foolish questions." Thinking his luck might still be in, and planning to push it, Rimbow said, "I'm going out back— fire a shot out the window as I go down the corridor, and three or four more during the next ten minutes. But don't do any more shooting after that unless they rush the front."

"You coming back?" Pinky asked, worried at the thought of being alone.

"Sure," Rimbow said. "Sure I'll be back."

Someone in front of the jail fired a double-barreled shotgun at the door, the consecutive blasts merging with a sharp rending of splintered wood, and now three rifles set up a continuing din, their positions revealed by wide-spaced blooms of muzzle flame.

When the firing died, someone in the crowd said apprehensively, "They keep that up, they'll get him sure."

Jim Rimbow heard the words, and was thinking the same thing as he crossed Main Street east of the sheriff's office and then walked along the south side of the dark thoroughfare. He had found surprisingly little vigilance at the back door of the jail—most of the crowd's attention was riveted to the front. He hoped Pinky Weaver knew enough to keep close to the floor. It occurred to Rimbow that he might break up the attack quickly by firing a few shots at shadowy shapes deployed in front of the jail. But the key culprits might escape, and he didn't want that to happen.

If it weren't for me, he thought, *there wouldn't even be a fight....* There was, he believed, a better than even chance of stopping the blow-up and fulfilling his obligation to Hawk Halliday into the bargain.

He slid quickly through the beam of window light in front of the Wells Fargo office and then quartered into pitch darkness beyond it. Pinky Weaver's arrival had changed his plans entirely; instead of waiting until Jardine's toughs decided to rush the jail he could do some attacking himself, and because they believed he was in the sheriff's office the Circle J trio should be wide open for a diversion from the rear.

Powder smoke was rank in the street and there was an

acrid smell of dust scuffed up by the boots of deploying attackers. He heard a man say, "Use the scattergun on that door again," and was trying to calculate the speaker's exact position, when guns began blasting, one so near that its muzzle flare gave Rimbow a fleeting glimpse of Kid Antrim's face.

The Kid was forted up behind a rain barrel, less than ten feet away.

Keeping Antrim's vague shape tightly focused, Rimbow stepped up behind him, jabbed his gun into the Texan's back and said quietly, "Keep still or I'll blow your backbone through your belly."

Antrim remained in a half crouch, as if frozen. Rimbow reached around with his left hand and snatched the rifle from his fear-sprung fingers. In a matter of seconds he had Antrim's right wrist shackled and his holster empty.

He said, "Call Zig Chisum over."

"To hell with that," Antrim objected sullenly.

It was, Rimbow understood, the courage of an unarmed man who considered himself out of the fight and thus safe from harm. The Kid had been badly scared a moment ago, while he still had a gun. Now he considered himself a prisoner.

And time was on his side.

There was another burst of firing from a nearby rifle. Rimbow moved the snout of his pistol and triggered a shot that ripped through Antrim's shirt just above the hip. Antrim gave a whimpering curse.

Rimbow warned, "Next one will take off some hide." He pressed the gun into a roll of flesh above the Kid's belt buckle and commanded rankly, "Call Chisum, damn you—call him!"

Antrim shouted, "Zig, come here!"

A nearby shape asked softly, "What you got in mind, Kid?"

Rimbow kept the pistol's snout tight as the shape loomed up and asked, "Is that you, Kid?"

"Yeah."

"What you want?"

"Come here."

"Who's that with you?"

The other was within three steps now. Rimbow said, "The law, Chisum—drop your gun."

"What the hell?" Zig blurted.

"Drop your gun," Rimbow said to Chisum.

Kid Antrim whined, "Don't do no shooting, Zig—he's got me in front of him."

Chisum cursed and dropped the rifle. Rimbow said, "Turn around," and prodded Antrim up to Chisum and snatched Zig's gun from its holster. Then, with a pistol pressed to each man's back he commanded, "Put the other cuff on him, Kid, and be damned quick about it."

When that was accomplished, Rimbow said, "Forward march," and walked them toward the jail office.

There was sporadic firing ahead of them and Antrim protested, "You'll get us all shot!"

Ignoring that, Rimbow prodded his prisoners past shadowy shapes and wondered how many of these attackers had any real interest in the fight. Some of them, he supposed, were merely spectators from the saloon crowd, made confident by the fact there'd been so little

166

shooting from the jail office—jackals, wanting in on the celebration when Nedrow was snatched from his cell.

Pinky Weaver felt the warm wetness of blood seeping from a wound on his right side, and understood that he was trapped. The front door was wrecked, one panel completely demolished and the top hinge gone, so that the door tilted against the bullet-shattered remnants of his desk. Rimbow had the back door key, so there was no escape in that direction. Now it was just a matter of time until the attackers would rush the office.

Like a rat in a trap, he thought morosely, and could scarcely believe that this was happening to him. It didn't seem possible; not to Pinky Weaver who had always contrived to take the safe side of any proposition. It seemed fantastic and beyond belief that he should be crouching here in a dark jail office beneath a shattered window, wondering if he dared to risk crawling through it. He, Pinky Weaver, pressing his hands tight against his bullet-slashed side; weak, and sick to his stomach, and thinking, *I'll bleed to death. . . .*

The sporadic firing continued, as did the harsh-toned voices. They seemed closer now, right outside the jail. Where was Rimbow? It seemed like a long time since Rimbow left, almost as if he'd never been here.

The thought came to Pinky that he could just lie still, pretending to be unconscious, when the shadows came. That would be the safe thing to do. Let them come in and grab the cell key ring and take Nedrow. They might not even notice him, over here by the window.

But even as the temptation took root in his mind, he remembered how relieved his wife had been at the thought that another man would take over the dangers of his job—subconscious shame had driven him into his clothes when the shots had awakened him. He remembered how proud she had once been of him—when they were first married——she'd never have spoken about him then as she had tonight to Rimbow.

Pinky Weaver picked up his pistol. A man who wore the star was responsible for the jail if it was attacked. Three bullets ripped through what was left of the door; in the abrupt silence that followed, Pinky thought: *Now they're going to make a rush!*

But instead a man outside yelled, "Quit shooting—quit shooting!"

Weaver was wondering about that when Jim Rimbow called, "Light the lamp, Pinky."

That made no sense to Weaver. "You mean now?" he asked. "Right now?"

"Yes, light it, quick."

In the time it took him to do that, Weaver was aware of a sudden and absolute hush out there in the street. No one seemed to be moving, or talking. Just a dead silence. Then, with the lamp lighted, he saw what was outside the demolished door.

It was a sight to see.

A sight to stare at in disbelief.

Zig Chisum, handcuffed to Kid Antrim, facing the street with Jim Rimbow standing behind them while vague shapes in the farther shadows stood motionless as statues.

"The fight's over," Rimbow announced, his voice ripping sharp as a rifle shot across the silent street. "Joe Bodine—I'm giving you until sunup to leave town. After that I'm shooting you on sight!" Then, not turning, he said quietly, "Shove that desk aside so we can come in, Sheriff Weaver."

And the way he spoke the last words made Pinky forget his wound. It made him feel proud.

15

This Star Says—Die!

NEXT MORNING Rimbow was up at his usual time. There had been the usual aftermath of questions and statements last night. Nedrow had been killed in his cell by a ricocheting slug, fired by one of his would-be rescuers, and Doctor Carter, acting as coroner, had just finished filling out a long form on Red Nedrow's demise when word came that another dead man was lying across the street—a bouncer from the Silver Dollar known simply as Bucko. The local correspondent for the Tombstone *Epitaph* had tried to pump Rimbow about his town-taming past in Abilene; failing in that he had accepted Rimbow's solemn assurance that the real hero was Sheriff Pinky Weaver who had defended the jail so courageously in spite of his wound. And Pinky, basking in the proud glow of his wife's eyes, had accepted a hero's role with the appreciation of a man savoring a new and soul-satisfying flavor.

The irony of Nedrow's death hadn't occurred to Rimbow last night. But now, as he went downstairs for breakfast, the thought came to him that Red's companions had accomplished a chore at which he had failed, that instead of freeing a friend they had executed a murderer—yet recalling how Nedrow had looked lying dead in his cell, Rimbow thought oddly that Red's face had held the same oddly impelling dignity as had Jube Tanner's, whom Red had killed.

Rimbow was eating breakfast when Lew Tiffany came into the dining room accompanied by Duke Hazelhurst and Billy Dial. They took a table nearby, only Hazelhurst speaking to him. Lew, Rimbow supposed, hadn't liked the outcome of last night's attempted jail break, even though he hadn't been directly involved. It had racked up another score for law enforcement and had, by the same token, weakened Tiffany's position as mayor of the riffraff element.

As if sharing a kindred thought, Tiffany got up and came to Rimbow's table and said, "I want to tell you something."

"Go ahead," Rimbow suggested.

Tiffany waited, as if wanting an invitation to sit down. When it didn't come he took a chair anyway, and there was a note of controlled anger in his low voice when he said, "I promised Marlene Lane I wouldn't get into a shootout with Mike O'Mara's partner. Because of that promise I took talk from you that no man should take from anybody."

"So?"

"I've told Marlene that the promise had nothing to do with a city marshal."

"You're wrong about that," Rimbow disagreed.

"What do you mean?" Tiffany demanded.

"Why, if it hadn't been for that promise and the way

you took my talk, meek as a lamb, I wouldn't have been hired as city marshal in the first place."

It obviously was a new angle to Tiffany; his amber eyes blinked, and secretly amused by the big man's momentary confusion, Rimbow said with mock appreciation, "You made me look like a killer marshal for sure, that day—like the stories those newspapers printed about me in Abilene."

Even now, with anger riding him, Tiffany's florid face retained its usual blandness. Only his voice revealed a rising tension as he said, "Whatever the results were, my promise had nothing to do with a Saturday night curfew—a damned spite curfew no other town in Arizona Territory has. And I'm telling you not to come into my place tonight unless there's a disturbance that calls for interference by a peace officer."

Rimbow wasn't surprised. Rather it was the lack of such an ultimatum earlier that had puzzled him. Tiffany was a horse-trader who seldom revealed his personal feelings; a businessman who calculated in dollars most of the moves he made. Any procedure that increased revenue was good, to Tiffany's way of thinking; conversely anything that cut revenue was bad. Tiffany had tried to trade five week-day curfews for one wide open Saturday night. Failing that he was now making a move to protect the stakes involved.

"You sound," Rimbow suggested, "as if the voters had elected you mayor of Reservation."

Tiffany's eyelids tightened, squeezing out the amber surfaces until only the black pupils were visible. Color stained his cheeks and briefly he was nearer to outright anger than Rimbow had ever seen him—in this moment Lew Tiffany revealed a side of himself that Rimbow had guessed about many times—his vulnerability to derision.

Abruptly Tiffany willed himself to calmness. The angry stain faded from his face. "I'm telling you to stay out of my place unless there's a legitimate reason for you to enter it," he said in the mildly contemptuous tone of a roundup boss talking to a greenhorn. "And I'm telling you there's nothing personal in it—nothing to do with the past. Just a matter of business. You understand?"

Rimbow nodded.

Tiffany sat a moment longer, as if expecting a verbal reaction; then he got up and walked back to his table in the leisurely fashion of a man finished with a trivial task.

The gambler's reference to Marlene Lane reminded Rimbow of the invitation he had rejected last night. A cup of coffee, she'd said, but the offer involved more than that. Thinking about it now he wondered why he had been so concerned about her morals. His resentment, he supposed, had something to do with the fact that Mike O'Mara had wanted her—that Mike had died for the privilege of kissing her. It occurred to him now that he should have accepted her invitation. He thought, *I should've taken what Mike didn't get. . . .*

Rimbow remembered what his father had said the night his mother had run off with a guitar-playing drifter: "There's no understanding them, son. You can live with one for fifteen years but all you know about her is that she's a woman."

173

A long time ago. A bitter, tragic time that he had never forgotten. . . .

Rimbow was having a smoke on the veranda when Eve Chastain drove a light ranch wagon into town, accompanied by a mounted escort of four riders. As they passed the hotel, Eve glanced at him and he thought she was going to halt the team. Her eyes, shaded by a fashionable, forward-tilted hat, gave him a speculative regard—then she smiled and called, "Good morning, Marshal Rimbow."

He lifted his hat in response and watched her drive to the hitchrack in front of Fritz Elmendorf's saddle shop. A Spade rider tied the team; another gave Eve a hand down, and still another lifted a saddle from the wagon and followed her into the shop with it. Observing this performance Rimbow thought: *A cattle queen and her outriders.*

Tiffany and Dial came out of the hotel lobby and went down the steps without looking at him. A woman and her teen-aged daughter passed, each peering briefly and almost boldly at Rimbow, as if compelled by an overwhelming inquisitiveness. A freckle-faced boy, trailing them by half a dozen steps, gawked in fascination, until called away by his mother.

Duke Hazelhurst came out to the veranda and stood at the steps while he lit a cigar. Not looking at Rimbow he said softly, "I hear that Joe Bodine is still in town. Watch out for him, friend Jim."

"*Gracias,*" Rimbow said. Covertly watching for the

effect, he announced, "Eve Chastain is in Elmendorf's place."

Hazelhurst glanced that way sharply. A quick smile animated his usually sober face and he said, "Thanks. Thanks very much." He walked hurriedly toward the saddle shop.

A clerk from the Mercantile came to the veranda steps now and said, "Mayor Martin wants to see you, Marshal."

Rimbow nodded and followed him to the Mercantile. Martin, he supposed, wanted assurance that the twelve o'clock curfew would be enforced tonight.

But it wasn't that at all. Closeted with the merchant in his office, Rimbow discovered a new facet of Martin's character; a facet he hadn't suspected. Martin pointed to five brand-new Winchesters propped against his desk and announced, "After what happened last night I've made up my mind we owe you some backing."

"We?"

"The Citizen's Committee. I'm going to load those guns and give one to each member. When you go to the Lady Gay tonight there'll be five guns backing you up."

It seemed fantastic to Rimbow; so unexpected that for a moment he just stood there staring at this meek-eyed merchant. Then he asked cynically, "To protect the town's five-hundred-dollar investment?"

"No, Jim—to protect Reservation against another such disgusting spectacle as occurred last night."

"Disgusting?"

Martin nodded. "A whole crowd of respectable citizens stood by while a few desperadoes staged an armed uprising against law and order. Your part in that spectacle was superb, and so was Pinky Weaver's. But it made the rest of us seem shamefully lacking in civic pride."

So that was it. This mayor had more gumption than showed on the surface. More courage, certainly, than most merchants possessed. And, Rimbow thought, more courage than ability. It was ability that counted in the clutch.

"Won't be necessary," Rimbow said.

"But it's being told around town that Tiffany will not close at midnight."

"He'll close, by twelve-fifteen at least."

"Why don't you want our help?"

"Because several people could get hurt, mostly committee members. Too many guns. Too many targets."

Martin seemed disappointed and relieved at the same time. "Perhaps you're right," he admitted. "None of us has had any experience at that sort of thing. Is there anything else we can do to help you?"

Rimbow shook his head. But presently, walking through the store with Martin, he said, "Yes, one thing. I hear Joe Bodine is still in town. If any of you see him, or find out where he's hiding, let me know. I'd like to settle with him before dark."

"We'll do it," Martin promised. "I'll have everyone keep watch for him."

Twice during the afternoon word came to Rimbow that Bodine had been seen, once going into the Silver Dollar, and again on Front Street. But each time his hurried response to the tips was in vain, and at five o'clock, with three rounds of the town completed, there had been no sign of Bodine.

Rimbow was sitting on the veranda at dusk when Eve Chastain came out of the lobby and took a chair beside him. "I heard about last night," she said. "I think you were wonderful."

Embarrassed by this praise from a girl whom he had disliked so heartily, and who had reciprocated that dislike, Rimbow said, "You can tell Halliday his prisoners are all accounted for."

"He'll be pleased, and so will dad. I guess you know that's the real reason Jeff came—as a favor to my father. Spade can take care of itself against ordinary riders, but Jardine imported professional gunmen."

"He's fresh out of them now," Rimbow said.

"Thanks to you, and Pinky Weaver, which seems surprising. I never thought Pinky would lift a hand against Jardine riders." Presently she said, "I guess you know about Duke and me."

Rimbow nodded.

"Well, we're going to Tombstone on the night stage and will be married there," she said, a barely controlled excitement in her voice.

"I wish you well," Rimbow said, mildly surprised that he could feel gracious toward this girl. "Duke is a fine man. One of the best."

Eve reached over and clasped his hand. She said happily, "I'm so glad you think that, Jim."

She was smiling at him when she said it, but Rimbow didn't see that; he was looking at Marlene Lane who walked past the veranda now with a shopping basket on her arm; a domestic looking Marlene in a gingham dress. She glanced at Eve, then at Rimbow and said, "Good afternoon, Marshal," and walked on without stopping.

Eve said, "Isn't it too bad about her, having to sing in a saloon to support a crippled husband."

"Yes," Rimbow agreed, but he wasn't thinking about that part of it. He was remembering how it had been when he had kissed Marlene.

Duke Hazelhurst came up the steps now. Despite Rimbow's demurrers, Duke insisted that he have supper with them. The poker dealer was more exhilarated and jovial than Rimbow had ever seen him as he said, "I've dealt my last card for Lew Tiffany."

"Lew take it hard?" Rimbow inquired.

Hazelhurst nodded. "Lew said that any man who would quit a high-pay job just to get married should have his head examined."

"I've already examined your head and I like it very much," Eve said smilingly.

Hazelhurst had chosen a table near a side window and to the rear. It was dusk when they finished supper. Rimbow stood up, and stepped aside so that Duke could escort Eve from the dining room.

At this moment a gun blasted outside the hotel window.

Drawing with an instinctive, reflex motion, Rimbow fired twice through the window screen. A woman at a nearby table screamed and Rimbow saw Eve down on her knees beside Duke Hazelhurst.

He ran through the kitchen and out into the back yard, listened for the sound of footsteps and heard none. But the faint smell of risen dust came to him, and he thought, *Crossed through here on his way to the alley.*

Going to the rear gateway, Rimbow stopped and thumbed a match to flame. The bootprints were plain in the dust.

Bodine, Rimbow thought, and knew that Hazelhurst had been hit by a bullet intended for himself.

Patiently then, with the methodical thoroughness of a man trained in the desperate game of gunman's hide-and-seek, Rimbow searched the dives, backyards and passageways of Burro Alley. It was after ten o'clock when he returned to the Palace and learned that Duke Hazelhurst, in a room upstairs, was given an even chance of living. The bullet had broken a rib and missed his heart by inches. Eve Chastain and Doc Carter were still with him.

Shortly before eleven o'clock Mayor Martin stopped by the Palace veranda and asked nervously, "Aren't you making a target for Bodine, just sitting there?"

Rimbow nodded. "I can't find him. Maybe he'll find me."

But a half hour passed, and then another half hour, and there was no sign of Bodine. Again, as he had a dozen times, Rimbow tried to think of a hiding place he hadn't investigated. He had looked into every back room, under every bed, at the Fandango and the girlie shack, and in the hotel on Front Street. The thought came to him that Bodine might have left town. But that didn't seem likely. A man like Bodine wouldn't quit until a job was done.

It occurred to Rimbow that Riley Jardine must be wondering what had happened to his four gunslingers. The Circle J boss, he supposed, was playing it smart. Jardine had left town before the attempted jail break and was playing it safe; no one could accuse him of direct involvement.

There was a big crowd in town tonight. Saddled horses and ranch rigs lined the hitchracks; thirsty men crowded Burro Alley and kept the Lady Gay batwings swinging. It was about time for Marlene to be coming across the street, and Rimbow wondered if she would again ask him in for a cup of coffee. Then he realized that he couldn't walk home with her; that the risk would be too great, with Joe Bodine gunning for him. But one of these nights she might ask him in and he would find out what kind of woman Mike O'Mara had died for kissing. When he looked at his watch it was eleven-thirty and Marlene hadn't come out of the Lady Gay. Perhaps she worked later on Saturday nights.

And where was Joe Bodine? Why didn't he make another try?

At eleven forty-five Monk Finucane and Fred Peppersall came up to the veranda, Monk saying, "By the sound of it they don't intend to close."

"Reckon not," Rimbow said, and flipped a half-smoked cigar into the street.

Mayor Martin came up with Cash Bancroft and asked, "Do you think Tiffany will put up a fight?"

"Hard to say," Rimbow said and walked across Main

Street in the leisurely fashion of a man going for a night-cap.

The four men in front of the hotel watched him in silence for a moment. Then Cash Bancroft said, "No nerves, no fear. Such men must be born like that—born to fight."

16

The Guns Speak Last

THE smoke-wreathed saloon fairly roared with a tumult
of loud talk and laughter, with the clack and clatter of
roulette and poker games. Men were ranked solidly at
the long bar; others whirled bare-shouldered girls on
the dance floor or crowded the gambling layouts. Lew
Tiffany had a capacity crowd this night, a big revenue
crowd.

"One seat open for a poker player!" shouted a dealer.

Lew Tiffany was at the faro table, standing behind
the dealer and intently watching the play. Rimbow was
within a few feet of the table when Tiffany looked up
and saw him. As if on signal now, the fat piano player
announced hurriedly: "Ladies and gentlemen—Marlene!"

She came to the piano at once, smiling acknowledgment of the applause that greeted her. This had been
perfectly timed, Rimbow thought cynically, and understood that his entrance had been the signal for her
appearance. While his eyes quested the room for sight
of Joe Bodine, Tiffany inquired, "A little early, aren't
you?"

Rimbow shook his head. There was one right way to

handle this—the quick way. Drawing his gun he took snap aim at a chandelier and fired. In the sharp hush that followed, he announced, "This place is closing down."

For a long interval the silence held. Dancers, who had ceased their cavorting in midstride, stood poised on the raised floor at the rear of the big room. Only the clack of an ivory ball in the still-whirling roulette wheel broke the strict hush until Lew Tiffany demanded, "What's the idea of smashing my fixtures?"

"Your lights are supposed to go out at twelve o'clock," Rimbow said. "Pay off now and close up."

"Suppose I don't?" the big gambler asked.

Rimbow waggled the gun at him, said, "You've got no choice."

Tiffany glanced about him as if seeking assurance from the crowd. "A real tough city marshal," he mused; then pushed back the lapels of his fancy vest. Blandly smiling, he asked, "You wouldn't shoot an unarmed man, would you?"

Guessing instantly what the gambler had in mind, Rimbow said, "No, I don't shoot unarmed cowards."

Tiffany chuckled, seeming to enjoy this. "Would you fight a coward with your bare fists?"

"Sure," Rimbow agreed at once. Prodded by a need for physical action he moved forward and said impatiently, "Come on—come on!"

As Tiffany stepped toward him, a drunken miner shouted gleefully, "Fight—fight!"

Rimbow swung at Tiffany's face and missed, then scored with a right to the big man's middle. Tiffany

183

grunted, but the blow didn't seem to jar him at all. He struck back, knocking Rimbow on his heels.

Billy Dial shouted, "Smash him down, Lew!"

Rimbow countered with a jab to the face and then targeted Tiffany's midriff with a sledging right. The big man scarcely moved; he swung his big fists boldly, and jolted Rimbow visibly each time he landed.

"Knock his head off!" a percentage girl shrilled, and now Tiffany announced, "I'll show you who's a coward, lawdog!"

Ducking a vicious uppercut, Rimbow took a right on the shoulder, whirled swiftly and caught Lew with a jab to the face. Not a hard blow, but because it landed between cheek and nostril, blood oozed from Tiffany's nose and that seemed to infuriate him. Bellowing a curse, he charged.

Instead of retreating, Rimbow blocked the first barrage of blows with both arms, then stood toe to toe with Tiffany, slugging and being slugged. It was a foolish thing to do, outweighed as he was; a loco, prideful thing. Jim Rimbow knew it; yet, because the thrusting need for vengeance was a bloodlust in him, he thought of only one thing—to smash down this gambler who had killed Mike O'Mara.

So, with a savagery that knew no caution, Rimbow slugged it out with Tiffany and, momentarily outgaming him, forced Tiffany toward the batwings. When the big man knocked him back with a blow to the face, Rimbow merely shook his head and pitched forward again. They were under the dangling remnants of the chandelier, their boots crunching broken glass, when

Tiffany's fists exploded in rapid succession against Rimbow's jaw.

For a blank moment Rimbow had no exact impression of what was happening. He didn't know he was down until broken glass cut his hands and knees. Then, as his senses cleared, he heard a woman cry: "No, Lew—no!" and barely dodged the boot that came at his face. He understood then that he was down and Tiffany was kicking him. He took a boot against a shoulder, then grabbed the boot in both hands, holding to it as he rose and spilling Tiffany whose head hit the plank floor with a resounding thud.

The big man was hurt. It showed in the slow way he got up, and in the blank expression of his eyes.

Rimbow targeted Tiffany's face with his right fist, waited for Lew's hands to lift instinctively to bashed nostrils, then slammed a right and left to the belly, knocking him backwards toward the batwing doors.

It wasn't far to the doorway. As if realizing that the batwings were a deadline, a symbol of utter rejection, Tiffany attempted to alter the course of his desperate retreat. But Rimbow, panting now and tired, still retained enough agility and power to have his way. Tiffany made a last stubborn stand with his back to the batwings; he took punishment and gave it. For an instant of frenzied in-fighting the smack of fists against flesh merged with the gusty breathing of two sweating men locked in no-quarter combat; then Tiffany backtracked out to the stoop.

With a sense of victory whipping up a savage eagerness in him, Rimbow hit Tiffany with both fists, and as the big gambler tilted over, grasped his torn and blood-stained shirt to steady him.

"This is for Mike O'Mara," he panted and then slugged Tiffany with a right to the face.

Tiffany fell backward off the stoop, his elbows thumping the plank walk. Dazed and blank-eyed in the shaft of light from the Lady Gay, he attempted once more to get up. He was on one knee and rising when Rimbow, deliberately measuring him, swung a hard right that landed just below the big man's ear.

That finished Tiffany.

He gave a long breath, went limp and lay still.

Rimbow wiped bloody knuckles on his pants. He turned to face Billy Dial who stood in the doorway. "Put out those lights," he ordered rankly, "or I'll put them out for you."

"Sure," Dial agreed, "soon as I tote Lew inside."

There was a considerable crowd in the street. A silent crowd which opened a lane for Jim Rimbow as he walked toward Burro Alley. A respectful crowd, regardless of individual affiliations, for even the riffraff who fear a city marshal's gunskill, and hate him for it, pay tribute to a man who wins with his fists against a bigger, heavier opponent.

Handsome Lew Tiffany had been cock-of-the-walk for many years in many towns. He did not look handsome, or cocky, as he was carried into the Lady Gay Saloon. . . .

One light showed in Burro Alley. Reckoning its

location, Rimbow thought: *The Silver Dollar*, and wondered why Blacky Pratt should so conspicuously disregard the curfew. He was a dozen steps in the alley when the answer came to him—Joe Bodine!

And at the same instant a gun blasted from across the alley.

The bullet burned across the upper muscle of Rimbow's right arm, but it didn't keep him from drawing. As the other gun set off a spurt of muzzle flare, he sent two fast shots at that brief beacon. Another bullet whined past Rimbow's head, breaking a window somewhere behind him. Rimbow side-stepped, fired again, and again stepped aside. Counting the bullets left in his gun, he thought: *Two more. . . .*

He stood listening.

There was no sound, save the indistinct murmur of voices out on Main Street. A warm wetness along his arm reminded Rimbow that Bodine's first slug hadn't missed by much; he thought: *The dirty sneak . . .* and searched the darkness for a target.

Mayor Martin called worriedly from somewhere behind him, "You all right, Jim?"

Rimbow remained silent.

That was a fool merchant for you, inviting a man to commit suicide.

He waited out another interval, then moved warily across the alley's dust. This was when a city marshal earned his pay, sweating out the final seconds of a fight. If Bodine didn't fire now he had run off again, or been knocked down. . . .

Then Rimbow detected the vague outline of a sprawled

shape on the hard-packed dirt walkway, and thought: *So I got him!*

He kept his gun ready as he moved in. A wounded man could play possum, waiting for a target he wouldn't miss. But the indistinct shape remained motionless as Rimbow thumbed a match aflame and peered into the slack-jawed face of Joe Bodine.

Mayor Martin called again, and when Rimbow answered there was the sound of many men moving into the alley. But it was Marlene Lane who came to Rimbow first, all out of breath and demanding, "Jim—are you hurt?"

"Just a scratched arm," Rimbow said. Recalling last night's invitation, he added, "Nothing a cup of coffee wouldn't cure."

"Then come have it." Marlene took his arm and he let her lead him through the gathering crowd. "I was so afraid you'd been shot."

"Not this time," Rimbow said, the subtle fragrance of her perfume enchanting him. This, he thought, would be a fitting finale to a tough night. An ironic finale. He had pounded down Lew Tiffany and was now going home with Lew's bonanza.

As if sharing that thought, Marlene said, "Duke told me you could lick Lew in a fist fight. That's why I wanted it that way, instead of with guns."

"You wanted it?" Rimbow demanded.

Marlene nodded. "I knew it had to come to a showdown between you and Lew. So I suggested he fight you with his fists, and he agreed to it."

Rimbow stopped and took her by the shoulders and

188

asked, "Were you afraid Lew might get shot, if we used guns?"

"No, Jim. Afraid—you might be shot."

Her face was a vague oval in the darkness, yet he sensed the wistful smile that would be on it. It was as if he knew her so well that he could feel her reactions; could know exactly how her eyes and her lips were shaped by what she felt at this moment. But the thought came to him now that he didn't know her at all—that no man could ever really know a woman. And hard on the heels of that realization came the bleak memory of his father's tragic bafflement, of Mike's death.

At Rimbow's whispering curse, Marlene asked, "What's wrong, Jim?"

"I'm wrong," he said flatly. "Wrong enough to want another man's wife. A cripple's wife."

She didn't speak, but something came from her to him; something lovely as the echo of remembered laughter, yet so impelling and so intimate that he took her in his arms.

"Do you really want me?" Marlene asked.

"Like I never wanted anything in my life," Rimbow said, and then he laughed, mirthlessly, with self-mockery. "For the first time I want a wife, and she's already married."

Marlene snuggled close to him. "I'm so glad," she whispered. "So very, very glad."

And then, with her arms tight about him, she said, "Bill isn't my husband, Jim. He's my brother."

"Your brother?"

"Yes."

189

"Then why are you wearing a wedding ring?"

"A trick to keep men from making love to me," Marlene explained, very sober about this. "It was Bill's idea, and it seemed a good one. But it didn't work with you."

For a moment Rimbow stood shocked by the knowledge that this woman was free, as he was free. Regretting his harsh judgment of her, he said humbly, "So that was why you let me kiss you."

Marlene laughed at him. "Not exactly," she teased. "There was another reason."

"So?"

"I liked the feel of your hands that first time you held me, in the Mercantile doorway. Remember? I wanted you to kiss me right then, in broad daylight."

"How about now?"

"Yes," she said, and her throaty voice held a sigh of satisfaction.

Leslie Ernenwein was born in Oneida, New York. He began his newspaper career as a telegraph editor, but at eighteen went West where he rambled from Montana to Mexico, working as a cowboy and then as a freelance writer. In the mid 1930s he went back East to work for the *Schenectady Sun*. In 1938 he got a reporting position with the *Tucson Daily Citizen* and moved to Tucson permanently. Later that year he began writing Western fiction for pulp magazines, becoming a regular contributor to *Dime Western* and *Star Western*. His first Western novel, *Gunsmoke Galoot*, appeared in 1941, and was quickly followed by *Kinkade of Red Butte* and *Boss of Panamint* in 1942. In addition to publishing novels regularly, Ernenwein continued to contribute heavily to the magazine market, both Western fiction and factual articles. Among his finest work in the 1940s are *Rebels Ride Proudly* (1947) and *Rebel Yell* (1948), both dealing with the dislocations caused by the War Between the States. In the 1950s Ernenwein wrote primarily for original paperback publishers of Western fiction because the pay was better. *High Gun* in 1956, published by Fawcett Gold Medal, won a Spur Award from the Western Writers of America, the first original paperback Western to do so. That same year, since the pulp magazine market had all but vanished, Ernenwein returned to working for the Tucson Daily Citizen, this time as a columnist. Ernenwein's Western fiction may be broadly characterized as moral allegories, light against darkness, and at the center is a protagonist determined to fight against injustice before he is destroyed by it. *Bullet Barricade* (1955), perhaps his most notable novel from the 1950s, best articulates his vision of how the life of man is not governed by a fate over which he has no control, even though life itself may seem like a never-ending contest against moral evil.